5.4

Monsieur Eek

Monsieur Eek

DAVID IVES

HARPERCOLLINS*PUBLISHERS*

Library of Congress Cataloging-in-Publication Data
Ives, David.
    Monsieur Eek / David Ives.
        p.   cm.
    Summary: When a chimpanzee arrives in MacOongafoondsen, he
is put on trial for being a thief and a French spy, resulting in some
changes to the tiny town that delight Emmaline Perth, his thirteen-
year-old defender.
    ISBN 0-06-029529-5 — ISBN 0-06-029530-9 (lib. bdg.)
    [1. Chimpanzees—Fiction.   2. Trials—Fiction.   3. Humorous
stories.]   I. Title.
PZ7.I1948 Mo   2001   00-044934
[Fic]—dc21   CIP
                                                              AC

1   2   3   4   5   6   7   8   9   10
❖
First Edition

*This book is dedicated to
David Berreby,
a fellow chronicler
of life in MacOongafoondsen*

We have met the enemy, and he is us.
—Pogo

Contents

Monsieur Eek

1

The Great Freeze

Spring was approaching, but the great coastal city of MacOongafoondsen (population 21) still lay coated with winter. Now on a midnight at the end of March of the year 1609, the vast metropolis— twelve houses, eighteen stables, and a tiny chapel— was so bleached by frost that if you looked down Only Street, the only street in town, you would have thought it had snowed.

The bone-white frost glowed so brilliantly you could clearly make out Fierfl the Tailor's tailor shop and Hammerklavver the Blacksmith's silent forge, which looked rigid with cold. You could even read the sign at Miss Darkniss the Candle Maker's that said DISMISS THE DARKNESS WITH MISS DARKNISS. Looking up to Old Castle Rock, looming bleakly over the town, you could detect the oppressive bulk of MacOongafoondsen Castle, where people said the crimson ghost of old Angus MacOongafoondsen walked, leaving its trail of fresh red drops of blood.

Far out at sea, winter was working up one last tantrum. If you stood on the beach now and looked west, you would've seen the approaching black wedge of the storm and heard thunder booming far away. But no one ever stood on that beach, because the citizens of MacOoongafoondsen were, by tradition, afraid of the sea. No one in town (except one person, as you will see) ever bathed in the ocean or even knew how to swim. No one was out tonight anyway except the city's resident philosopher, a marsh owl who wondered aloud, *Who's who? Who's who?"* but got no answer.

Only one of Miss Darkniss's excellent candles burned tonight in the great coastal city of MacOongafoondsen. It glowed behind the closed shutters of a tumbledown shop at the far end of town, where Only Street petered out into MacOongafoondsen Marsh. A sign hanging from the front of the shop swayed and creaked on its hinges and said, simply, SHOP.

"So the defense rested," a young man was saying, "in the trial of Erik the Ax Maker versus Wingamore the Bird Catcher."

Inside the shop, a young man in a visored rainbow-colored cap hunched for warmth at a small table, reading aloud from an enormous ancient book. Next to him huddled a girl, who had to sit on another enormous ancient tome so she could be high enough to see the page, her feet dangling inches off the cold stone floor. The single thin candle on the table was the only light and warmth in the room. The breaths of the boy and girl steamed in the air, mingling in a single flame-tinted cloud of mist over the book.

"The jury voted guilty," the boy read on, "and the court adj—the court adj . . ." He hesitated over a word. The girl next to him blew the long brown bangs out of her eyes to see the page better.

"Adjudicated," she said.

"*Adjudicated.* I should've gotten that one. Thanks, Emmaline. Boy, some of these words are difficult. They're formidable. Challenging. Abstruse."

"They're hard," the girl smiled. She knew that

3

her friend could never resist finding a list of long and complicated words for one short, simple one.

"They're very hard," he said. "Especially the polysyllabic, sesquipedalian ones."

Emmaline Perth was teaching Young Flurp the Town Fool to read. The huge tome on the table was one of her father's ancient law books. Emmaline was thirteen, proud of her Perth nose, ashamed of her big feet, and liked to be called Emma-*line*, not Emma-*leen*, because she thought Emma-line sounded more distinguished.

Until recently, this shop had been an abandoned stable with a couple of small rooms over it. The place still looked and smelled more like a stable than a shop, and the only items for sale were three wrinkled turnips, a door handle, and one left shoe. Until recently, Emmaline and her mother, Jane, had lived in the mayor's house at the other end of town. The Perths had been the first family of MacOongafoondsen, as Emmaline's father had been the town mayor, doctor, lawyer, and generally the wisest man in MacOongafoondsen all in one. Gabriel Perth had always been too busy helping people to make any money, so when he died unexpectedly, Emmaline and her mother had to sell all they had and move here, to the bad end of Only Street. Until recently, Emmaline's clothes had been fine-woven and bright; now they were scratchy-rough, and the color of earth.

"The court *adjudicated*," Young Flurp the Town Fool continued, savoring the word, "that Erik the Ax Maker had grievously insulted the law."

"Bravo," Emmaline let out.

"How's that for a beautiful phrase? *Grievously insulted the law*. Wow!"

Young Flurp did not look like you might expect a town fool to look. At fifteen, he was a handsome and well-formed youth, whose only defect was a pair of brilliant blue eyes, of a deep and flawless azure. Nobody in all MacOongafoondsen had blue eyes except members of the Flurp family, so the townsfolk thought Young Flurp looked somewhat *strange*. Then there was that rainbow-colored cap, which Young Flurp had made himself and which he wore everywhere. It was of a bizarre design unknown in MacOongafoondsen, and the populace thought it exotic, quirky, foreign—*weird*. The cap was shaped like this:

Young Flurp had other bizarre habits, like taking two pieces of bread, slavering them with mustard or mayonnaise, loading the bread with pieces of meat and cheese, lettuce and tomato, and eating this monstrosity for lunch. (People just shook their heads and said, "Town Fool.") In any case, because of their blue eyes, the Flurps had always been the town's fools, and now Young Flurp, with his outlandish headgear, had inherited the title.

"Read on?" he asked.

"Read on," Emmaline said. "It gets even better."

Flurp was Emmaline's best—or rather, only—friend in MacOongafoondsen. When Emmaline started teaching him to read, the first word Flurp learned was *Philip*, which was his real family name and which over generations of townfooldom had deteriorated into Flurp. Now Flurp was in love with words. He made lists of words, then lists of his lists, then lists of words for the word *list*. Sometimes for his lesson, he'd bring Emmaline a bouquet of goose quills as a gift, presharpened for writing.

Though everyone called him "Young" Flurp, he was the only Flurp there was, since both his father and his mother were dead. That made a bond between him and Emmaline. One of their favorite pastimes was to sit together and remember everything they could about their lost parents. Emmaline might recall how her father loved the word *spectacular*. "This tansy pie," he might say, "is spec-*tac*-ular." Or "What a spec-*tac*-ular Tuesday." Once, just before he died, Gabriel Perth had said to his daughter, "Emmaline, when I'm gone, always remember that your mother is a spec-*tac*-ular woman."

"Emmaline," a woman's voice called from upstairs. "Are you there?" The voice was thin, fragile.

"Yes, Mother," the girl called back. "I'm here with Flurp. We're reading."

"Don't you go outside."

"I won't, Mother."

"Don't go anywhere without telling me," the voice called weakly.

"I won't," the girl repeated.

Outside, the wind let out a cry. The SHOP sign creaked and all the shutters up and down Only Street banged like gavels. The owl in the marsh again wondered, *"Who's who? Who's who?"* and still got no answer.

"A storm's coming up," Flurp observed, and was about to continue reading when Emmaline interrupted.

"Flurp," she ventured thoughtfully, "have you ever wanted to live someplace else?"

"Someplace else? You mean other than MacOongafoondsen? What kind of place?"

"Maybe," the girl said, "a place where you didn't know everybody who lived in the place. A place larger than twenty-one people."

"Twenty-one seems pretty large to me," Flurp said. "Quite sizable. Even multitudinous. And they're all good people in this town. Well," he corrected himself quickly, *"mostly* good people."

"I don't even care if they're good people or not!" Emmaline exclaimed, blowing the bangs out of her eyes. "It's like . . . well, it's like my name."

"Your name?"

"What's my name?" she demanded.

"Well," Flurp said after a moment, "isn't it Emmaline?"

"Of course it's Emmaline! Or is it Emma-*leen*?"

"You hate it when people call you Emma-*leen*."

"But nobody ever does! Why? Because everybody in MacOongafoondsen, all twenty-one people, know I like to be called Emma-*line*, not Emma-*leen*. Every night I lie in bed and I hear that old owl going, *'Who's who?'* and I think, What a stupid question. In this town, *everybody* knows who's who! My father told me there are cities in the world with over a thousand people in them. You wouldn't know who's who in a city like that. You'd have to find out!"

"I'd sure hate to see you go live someplace else," Flurp admitted, "I mean, us being best friends and all. But if you ever did want to go to someplace larger, I say go. Not that I know how you'd get there. Who knows where the next city is. Who knows if there really *is* a next city. The rest of the world's just hearsay, from here."

9

Emmaline's shoulders sagged and she sank in her chair.

"Oh, it's not the size of the place, especially. It's just . . . Well, how's anything important ever going to happen in a city of twenty-one people? I mean, how could anybody ever do anything significant in a city of twenty-one people? I guess that's my problem. I'd like to do something really *significant* someday."

The wind interrupted the girl, rattling the door as if demanding entrance.

"I wish this storm would blow something significant our way," Emmaline muttered as if in prayer.

Little did she know.

2

Trapped at Sea

"Haul in the sheets!" the captain screamed. "Fore tops'l!"

Out in the middle of the Great Northern Ocean, while Emmaline and Flurp sat reading, winter's last storm was tearing up the sea as if it were a cobble-stoned road. In the heart of the tempest, the three-masted *Justice* struggled to stay afloat. Bearded with ice, bombarded by hail, the ship careened up and down long, steep, watery slopes among mountainous waves while lightning blasted the air overhead in thundering volleys. Sailors skittered over the ship's bobbing decks like mice.

"Up, men!" shouted the *Justice*'s captain, waving the sailors to the masthead. "Take in!"

Before anyone could start up the lines, the captain looked up and saw the screaming wind tear the last sails into rags. "Hard a lee!" he yelled to the man at the wheel.

Miguel de Parrìa, the sturdy pilot of the *Justice,* dragged all his weight and strength against the tiller, but the helm would not budge. He braced his feet and tried again, then felt the helm start to give way when, with a deafening crack, the mainmast snapped and crashed part on the deck, part in the sea. At the same moment, the sea bit the whole rudder off and the tiller went limp in the pilot's grip. It clicked and chattered in its chocks like the teeth in the mouth of a freezing sailor. The ship was now a mere twig in a whirlpool.

Suddenly with a *whoomp,* the whole main hatch cover flipped up and twirled off into the dark like a hat off a man's head. Tons of cold ocean poured into the ship's hold. The *Justice* rolled over and started to founder.

"Abandon ship!" the cry went up, and from all over the vessel, sailors fought their way toward the two small lifeboats lashed amidships. Only Miguel stood his ground.

"To the pumps!" Miguel shouted to a fleeing sailor. "We can still save her!" But the panicked

sailor ran on to help unlash the boats. "Go back!"
the pilot called to his mates, but they all pushed past
him, shoving him out of their way.

Meanwhile, the ship's only passenger was im-
prisoned belowdecks, his cries for help drowned out
by the deafening storm.

Locked in his cabin and forgotten, Samuel was
frantically rattling his door and tugging the handle,
but the bright red door was latched in the passageway outside, and no one on that boat could hear
Samuel's cries. How could they, when the entire
universe seemed to be screaming for help?

Three feet above Samuel's head, up on deck,
Miguel struggled against the wind to where the
captain was climbing over the rail to join the men in
the boats below.

"We can still save her, sir!" Miguel shouted.
"The *Justice* can weather this!"

But even the captain had given up hope.
"Abandon, Miguel!" he screamed in the pilot's ear.
"Forget the *Justice*! Save yourself!"

The captain dropped over the side and landed in
one of the boats. The sailors had scrambled over,
every man for himself, so now the other lifeboat had

too many men. Water was already lapping over its low gunwales. The men bailed frantically with their caps, but the boat was filling faster than they could bail.

Still, Miguel hesitated at the rail.

"Wait for me!" he shouted to the men below. "I'm going to get Samuel!" Gripping whatever he could, the pilot struggled back up the tilted, slippery deck toward the hatch that led below.

In one of the boats, a sailor grabbed the captain's arm. "Forget Miguel!" the sailor yelled.

"We have no time!" shouted another.

"Look!" screamed a third, pointing up at a coal-black wall of water toppling onto their heads. In a moment, the wave crashed down on the ship and the two small boats alike. When the captain looked again, the boat with too many men was gone and Miguel had disappeared, too, swept off the deck and into the sea.

"To the oars!" shouted the captain. "Away!"

The men pulling frantically, the minuscule craft drew off into the night to find its own way in the storm, then disappeared into the icy darkness.

Meanwhile, in that cabin belowdecks, the abandoned Samuel still futilely rattled that locked red door. He did not realize he was now completely alone on board the *Justice*.

3

A Change in the Weather

Ten mornings later, spring finally uncoiled in the great coastal city of MacOongafoondsen, population twenty-one. Violets emerged alongside Ongka the Fat Bread Maker's fragrant bakehouse. Purple crocuses shot up overnight around the Grogniks' tavern, where Tim and Tom, the twin Grogniks, were cooking up their famous pickled samphire and tansy pie. Buds began to burst on the birch trees below the old castle, where walked the crimson ghost of Angus MacOongafoondsen. And yellow daffodils covered Edge of the Sea Hill, where right now, if you looked, you could see Young Flurp the Town Fool running into view at the top, waving his rainbow fool's cap.

"A ship! A ship!" the young man was shouting as

he half stumbled, half rolled wildly down the slope of Edge of the Sea Hill to where the great city lay nestled at its bottom.

"Boat traffic!" he called. "A watercraft! Shiver me timbers, it's an ocean liner! A sailing vessel! A three-sticker! A packet ship! Call out the navy! Call out the merchant marine! Ahoy! Ahoy!"

Of course, there was no navy or merchant marine in MacOongafoondsen. The whole town harbored not a rowboat, raft, skiff, canoe, coracle, kayak, dory, pinnace, or punt, since the citizens of MacOongafoondsen traditionally feared the sea. The tradition dated from the very founding of MacOongafoondsen, when thirty travelers had landed on the beach here, driven ashore by a storm. After such a close escape, the pilgrims had turned their backs on the fearsome sea and never looked round.

"The fleet's in! Anchors away!"

Flurp was now crying his news while running up and down Only Street. "The foreigners are coming!" he cried joyfully. "The foreigners are coming!"

At the word *foreigners,* doors and shutters flew open all up and down Only Street—except in the

Perth shop, at the very far end. Behind its closed shutters, Emmaline was hunched over one of her father's law books, as usual. In one limp hand she held a hazel-twig broom. Every few minutes she'd absentmindedly blow the brown bangs out of her eyes and sweep the broom over an inch or two of floor, but her eyes were fixed on a page.

In a margin of that page, in her father's neat script, were written these words: "Justice is nothing but the science of being fair." She ran her fingertip over the old words. It was like touching her father's warm, living hand again. When she took her finger away, particles of dried ink came off as flakes on the pad of her finger. She rubbed them against her thumb as if she were rubbing mint leaves there to release their perfume.

"Emmaline," her mother's voice called from upstairs. "Are you there?"

"Yes, Mother," the girl called back.

"Are you sweeping?"

"Yes, Mother!" she said, and raked the broom over the stone floor a couple of times for the sound effect.

"Don't go out without telling me," the thin voice called.

Emmaline's mother had changed terribly since the death of Gabriel Perth. Once energetic, attractive, and vital, now careworn, her hair uncombed, Jane Perth spent most of her time in bed, as if she were crippled by some persistent, unnamed illness. Emmaline could not remember the last time she had seen her mother laugh or even smile. Certainly not since the death of Gabriel Perth. Worst of all for Emmaline, losing her husband had made Jane anxious that she might lose her daughter, too, so she kept Emmaline near home and seldom out of earshot. This had made for some prickly quarrels recently between mother and daughter.

"A ship! A ship!"

Emmaline's head popped up from her book. She thought she'd heard Flurp's voice, shouting in the street. Suddenly, there was a loud rap on the closed shutters. Emmaline jumped up and opened them to find Flurp standing right outside, his sky-blue eyes wide with wonder.

"Emmaline!" he said. "It's a frigate!"

With that mysterious announcement, he ran away up the street. All the citizens of MacOonga-foondsen were pouring—or rather, trickling—out of their houses.

"Mother!" Emmaline called toward the dark at the top of the staircase. "I think something's actually happening!"

"Don't you go anywhere," her mother's voice called. "Emmaline, do you hear me?"

Emmaline saw that the crowd had surrounded Flurp, who was now standing on the edge of the town well and gesticulating wildly with his hands. The crowd at the well seemed to be growing excited at whatever he was telling them. Emmaline heard voices being raised, and shouts.

"Mother," she called, "this might even be something *significant!*"

Emmaline leaned the twig broom inside the door and, without waiting for permission, dashed off toward the well.

4

A Town Meeting

"It's a boat as big as a house!" Flurp was saying when Emmaline reached the edge of the crowd. "It's enormous! Capacious! Colossal! Monumental! Mammoth!"

Just about all of MacOongafoondsen had gathered at the well. Emmaline saw Fierfl the Tailor, and Minister Moonster the Minister (who was Plain Willum the Weaver on weekdays), and Barbara the Carpenter and Luigi the Carpenter's Husband, and Akmed the Cobbler and his wife, Peaches, and Bob the Milkmaid and Miss Darkniss the Candle Maker, and Hammerklavver the Blacksmith alongside his sweetheart, Ongka the Fat Bread Maker, who was actually thin and shapely but made fat breads.

"Where lies this ship, Young Flurp the Town

Fool?" called out Kawasaki the Left-Handed Farmer.

"On the beach at the bottom of Edge of the Sea Hill, Kawasaki the Left-Handed Farmer," answered Flurp. "The great storm must have blown it there."

"Make way for the law!" somebody called out. *"Make way for the law!"*

Shmink the Bailiff now pushed his way through the crowd. Mr. Shmink wore his usual greasy black swallow-tailed coat and his bailiff's hat with the official sign of his office, a dead sparrow, on the brim. The sparrow had been dead for some time, and did not look happy about it.

"What's all this, then?" demanded Shmink. "Civic disorder? Inciting trouble, are you, Young Flurp the Town Fool? Or is someone else behind this insurrection?"

Shmink fixed his eye on Kawasaki's beautiful wife, Kareesha, as if she had done something wrong. "What is this gathering of the masses? Disperse, every one of you, instantly!"

"But Mr. Shmink," gushed Flurp, "there's a ship on the beach at the bottom of Edge of the Sea Hill."

"A ship?" Shmink snapped. "How do you know it's a ship?"

This was actually a good question, since nobody in MacOongafoondsen had ever seen a ship, the citizens being fearful of the sea. "Thy grandfather was town fool and thy father was town fool," continued Shmink, who sometimes liked to *thee* and *thou* people just because it sounded good. "How is a town fool from a family of fools to recognize a ship?"

"Well," Flurp said, "the thing is large and wooden and it seems to have come out of the sea, so I thought—"

"I'll do all the thinking around here," Shmink rapped out. "What were you doing at the sea in the first place? Dost thou think the ocean is any of thy business?"

"I wanted to look—"

"Oh, you wanted to *look,* eh?"

"Well, Edge of the Sea Hill was so beautiful this morning. . . ."

"I'll do all the looking around MacOongafoondsen." Shmink the Bailiff narrowed his eyes and again cast them around the crowd of people, as if one of them might have put the ship on the beach. "Who knows what I might find if I did a little looking, eh? Maybe I'd find some of those *things,* those missing *things,* those fine objects that've disappeared lately around our great city."

Shmink whipped a scroll out of his pocket, flipped it open with a flourish, and fixed it half an inch from his left eye.

"Wanted for Thievery," he proclaimed. "One Unknown Thief, Name Unknown, Description Unknown, Address Unknown. Other Information, Unknown. Said Thief has stolen one goose, roasted and stuffed."

"That were our goose," said Peaches Cobbler, raising her hand.

"One woolen sweater, red, with a spot of fried egg on the front," Shmink continued.

"That were my red sweater," said Bob the Milkmaid, raising a hand.

The scroll that Shmink held in his hand was actually blank, with no writing or printing on it of any kind, the only marks being Shmink's oily fingerprints. Like most of the other citizens of MacOongafoondsen, Shmink the Bailiff could not read, so he used this empty scroll to stand in for all official documents.

"Don't forget the cup," called out Luigi the Carpenter's Husband. "Golden and bejeweled."

"And one cup, golden and bejeweled," Shmink feigned reading from the empty parchment.

"That cup were the chapel's cup," Minister Moonster the Minister said firmly, raising his hand. "It were bejeweled with rubies and amethysts and emeralds and turquoise, and it were sacred, as well. So cursèd be the base villain who took it."

"Thank you, Reverend, I'll do all the cursing around here," snapped Shmink the Bailiff, rolling up the scroll quickly, as if everybody in town did not know it was blank.

There had not been a burglar in MacOongafoondsen in living memory, so these recent thefts had much disturbed the town. Emmaline especially wondered why anyone would steal the golden chalice from the chapel. You could not sell it to anyone in town, for then everyone would know you had stolen it. And you couldn't sell it to anyone outside of town, because nobody in town ever left the town.

"Bailiff, what are we going to do about this ship on our public property?" demanded Barbara the Carpenter.

"Might it really be foreigners?" asked Tom or Tim, one of the Grognik twins. "What do you think, Mr. Shmink?"

"What do *I* think?" said Shmink. "*I* think . . ." He paused a moment. "I think it's the French."

"The *French*!" everybody cried.

Emmaline felt a thrill at the words. The mysterious ship not only might have people she didn't know and who didn't know her; the people might even be French people. Her father had told her France was a great and powerful nation and its people ate fish eggs wrapped in paper-thin pancakes and wore lace on their sleeves and drank a bubbly wine called champagne. Or was it shampoo?

"Why the French?" asked Young Flurp the Town Fool, who preferred things to be logical.

"Why *not* the French?" snapped Shmink. "Blue-eyed fool! This so-called ship—if it *is* a ship—is not from here. Therefore, it must be foreign. If it's foreign, then the people on it—if there *are* people on it—must be foreigners. If the people on it are foreigners and the French are foreigners, therefore the people on it must be French!"

Before anybody could think about this too hard, Shmink raised the official tin trumpet he wore around his neck and blew a few squealing notes.

"Make way for His Honor the Mayor and his wife!" he proclaimed.

The crowd parted and Ignoratius B. Overbite and his wife, Lucretia, appeared, a puffy, jowly, overfed pair, still in their nightshirts and slippers. Overbite had been elected mayor after the death of Gabriel Perth. Since he was easily the most foolish person in all MacOongafoondsen (just as his wife, Lucretia, was the greediest), some people suspected the election had been fixed and the ballots switched by Shmink, but no one had ever proved it. Emmaline found it hard to look at this couple who had taken over the house she was brought up in and who now sat on the chairs she had sat in and ate off the plates she'd eaten off of as a little girl. Lucretia Overbite had bought all the Perths' household effects at insulting prices.

"What's all this, Mr. Shmink," demanded Mayor Overbite. "A riot? An uprising? A revolution?"

"No, sir," Shmink said, saluting off the dead sparrow on his hat. "It's the French, sir."

"But these people are not French," Mayor Overbite said, looking around the crowd. "I know every one of these people. That's Kawasaki the Left-Handed Farmer. That's Onderdonk the Very Tall Woodcutter. . . ."

"Not *these* people, sir," Shmink said through gritted, pitted yellow teeth. "The French have landed in the cove. Probably the first wave of a sea invasion. And you know what you have to do," he said pointedly.

"Surrender," the mayor said promptly.

"No," said Shmink.

"Move away?"

"No," said Shmink.

"Ship them back!" cried Mrs. Overbite.

A few people in the crowd picked up the cry.

"Ship them back! Ship them back!"

"Wait!" commanded Mayor Overbite. "Wait! In order to ship them back, we must go where they are first! Grab your weapons, men! Then everybody to the ship!"

"To the ship!" everybody cried.

The crowd started away up the street. Emmaline was about to follow, when she felt a pair of hands descend on her shoulders from behind, holding her back.

"Emmaline," her mother's voice said, "you went off without permission. You left the shop unattended."

"You were there to watch it," the girl protested, turning to her mother. "Anyway, there weren't any customers. Everybody was here."

Jane Perth tugged her black widow's shawl tighter around her shoulders. The woman looked pale and seemed to sag under the black shawl's weight. "You know I don't like you going off without permission. Something could happen to you."

"I *am* sorry," Emmaline said, "but a town meeting was on. A ship has landed and it might be the French! Can't I go see it, Mother?"

Her mother shook her head firmly. "No."

"Please, Mother."

"Let the child go to the ship," a fulsome voice said behind them.

It was Shmink the Bailiff, who had doffed his official hat, revealing the four oily strands of hair plastered across his pasty forehead. He tried tucking Emmaline's chin in his clammy hands, but she pulled away. His fingernails were ringed with tarlike filth.

"The girl means no harm," he said. Then, attempting a smile but achieving a leer, he took Jane Perth's clean hand in his soiled one and kissed it, imprinting a smudge on its back. "Kind lady," he crooned.

"All right, Emmaline," her mother sighed in an exhausted voice. "You may go."

"Thank you, Mother."

Skirting the bailiff, Emmaline ran up Only Street, past the mayor's house, which she avoided looking at, to the bottom of Edge of the Sea Hill, where she abruptly halted. The unexpected smell of violets had stopped her, and the blazing yellow of the daffodils blanketing the slope above. Emmaline took in the wide lapis lazuli sky overhead, which had not a single cloud in it. Hummingbirds and bumblebees bombinated all around her. She saw that all the trees were about to explode into green.

Emmaline realized that once again spring had come out of nowhere to MacOongafoondsen, and she hadn't even noticed. She stood a moment longer, inhaling all of spring's moist, promising odors, then ran on and caught up with Flurp, who was already halfway up Edge of the Sea Hill.

5

The Mystery Ship

"It's an adventure, isn't it?" said Flurp to Emmaline as they climbed. "It's an expedition. An exploit. A thrill."

"A lark!" Emmaline said.

"Exactly!" Flurp exclaimed. "It's a lark!"

"I mean," said Emmaline, pointing, "there's a lark."

Flapping up from a thornbush was the first lark she had seen that year. The bird fluttered around them, singing as if it were trying to tell them something, then flew away ahead of them and disappeared over the top of the hill, toward the sea.

"There it is!" a couple of voices cried in chorus. *"The ship!"*

It was Tim and Tom, the Grognik twins, standing atop the hill and pointing down its unseen side. Everybody rushed up the last stretch. Flurp grabbed Emmaline's hand and they ran up together, ahead of the others. As they ascended, the breeze grew stronger and stronger and turned into a real wind the moment they crested the hill. Then the ground suddenly gave way at Emmaline's feet and she found herself standing with her toe tips at a cliff's edge. Only Flurp's grip kept her from flying over.

"Oh, *my!*" Emmaline exclaimed when she saw the sea spread out to the horizon before her, the rippling, silken silver-blue Great Northern Ocean. Like most MacOongafoondsians, Emmaline rarely saw the sea and tended to forget its beauty and remember its fearsomeness. "Spec-*tac*-ular!" she breathed.

A seagull now swooped and hovered before the girl, almost in arm's reach, as if that land lark had transformed itself into a seabird. The gull hovered, hovered, hovered before the girl, then plummeted, gliding dizzily down the side of the cliff toward the cove below. When Emmaline saw what lay beached on the sand there, she said again, "Oh, *my!*"

It was the ship.

Emmaline had expected something forbidding, something sinister, but the ship seemed more like a giant, pretty toy. True, it looked battered by the storm, and the mainmast had cracked in two, and only tattered remnants of sails hung from what had been the crosstrees. But the graceful hull was painted bright blue-green up to the waterline and white above that all the way to the red rail. Brass fittings and the compass near the wheel gleamed brilliant gold in the sun.

More and more people joined her, until the entire population of MacOongafoondsen stood together at the top of Edge of the Sea Hill regarding the ship. Even Emmaline's mother joined the group, last of all, her heavy black widow's shawl rippling on her shoulders in the salty sea wind.

"Sinister, is it not?" said Mayor Overbite.

"Of course the ship is sinister," his wife said. "It's French. It's evil."

"Fearful," said Fierfl, visibly trembling.

"I think it's *gorgeous!*" Emmaline said.

"Beautiful," Flurp agreed, always ready with a word list. "Lovely. Splendid. Handsome. Pulchritudinous."

Kareesha Kawasaki whispered, "No sign of any people."

The crowd waited in silence a moment, as if to see whether any life would appear on board, but the gulls pecking on the deck and the rags of sails blowing in the breeze were the only moving things.

"The cowardly French are probably waiting to ambush us," Shmink the Bailiff said in a low tone. "Keep your weapons at the ready, men. Let's go. Women and young people first, as a shield."

Emmaline sprang forward to lead the way, heading off toward her left, where Edge of the Sea Hill descended in soft dunes to the water. Flurp followed her; then came the women, followed by the men in a snaky line. Weapons of any kind were unknown in MacOongafoondsen, so the men carried rakes and shovels and roasting spits and a chair and even an old feather duster. Mayor Overbite secretly kept his white handkerchief ready in case he needed to wave it and signal surrender.

On the way down, her feet slipping and sifting her down the sandy slope, Emmaline felt her heart pounding in the side of her throat. Soon she got far down enough that, when she licked her lips, she could taste salt. Then she was far down enough to hear the rattling of the pebbles on the shingle being sucked back and forth by the surf. Then she was standing on the harsh sand itself. The ship looked enormous and much less beautiful here, looming up ahead. A wave of frigid water washed over her feet, chilling and startling her.

She turned and saw everyone looking at her, as if expecting her to keep leading. Flurp took her hand again and the two moved forward slowly together. Emmaline called up the cradlesong her father had sung to her when she was a baby, and now, to steady herself, she hummed it over and over in her mind:

Cowbells and bluebells and church bells
Hear how they ring
Cowbells and bluebells and church bells
Hear how they sing
Happy day, happy day.

Emmaline and Flurp stopped where the dark purple shadow of the boat fell on the sand like a bruise. If she had taken two more steps, she could have touched the blue-green side of the hull with her hand. Far above her, painted in gold on the ship's prow, was a single stern word: *Justice*.

"You're doing well, girl," Shmink's voice whispered in her ear. "Go on."

But there was no way up to the deck. The wooden rungs in the side of the hull were far beyond anyone's reach. The sea that dropped the *Justice* here must have been high and powerful, for the ship lay completely out of the water and well above the tide line.

"I'll go," Flurp said quietly. He grabbed a loose rope dangling from the bowsprit, tested it, and ascended it nimbly, hand over hand. Hooking a leg over the rail, he swung over and dropped out of sight. Emmaline could hear the soft thud of his bare heels on the deck above. The great ship echoed his steps, booming like a drum. Then there was silence.

She was about to call out Flurp's name, when his head appeared at the rail right over them. He wordlessly motioned everybody back and lowered the remains of a torn rope ladder down the side. Emmaline was the first one up. She had to climb carefully, because the soggy seaweed sticking to the twisted rungs was slick. When she reached the rail—*squawk!*—a gull shot right up at her and the girl flew backward off the ladder. Flurp grabbed her arm in time and helped her onto the deck, then ushered the others on board, until all twenty-one citizens of MacOongafoondsen were standing on the deck of the *Justice*. Not a word had been spoken. Nobody moved.

6

Emmaline Explores

The deck was littered with debris. Sand and shells and driftwood and dead fish lay heaped at the rails. Shmink the Bailiff picked up a twisted, waterlogged pink-and-green-dotted cloth, using the salad tongs he was carrying as a weapon. He mouthed the words *French flag* to the others, though he had never seen a French flag and had no idea what the French colors were. "French flag, French flag" was murmured from mouth to mouth.

Emmaline, meanwhile, had begun to think all this sneaking about silly.

"Hello!" she cried out. "Anybody home?"

"SHHHHHHHHH!" went all the citizens of MacOongafoondsen at once.

"We're friends!" she called even louder. "Olly olly oxen free!"

"Be quiet, child!" Shmink shouted.

"Obviously, there's nobody here," the girl said to him. "And we *are* friendly. Aren't we?"

"But who knows if *they* are!" reasoned Shmink, in a low scream.

Mr. Overbite decided that now was the time to assert his office, since his wife was hissing and motioning to him. He stood on a fat dead mackerel to make an official announcement, though he was still in his nightshirt and slippers.

"This is Ignoratius B. Overbite, the mayor of the great coastal city of MacOongafoondsen!" he proclaimed, although not too loudly. "I command you to show yourselves and surrender! But let me warn you, we are heavily armed!" He himself was carrying an old limp leather belt for a weapon, which he now brandished fiercely. "This is your last chance!"

Mr. Shmink yelled, *"Fire!"* but as the town had no guns, the men just raised their weapons in a threatening, gunlike manner.

Since nobody returned fire and the only sounds were still those of the wind, the surf, and the gulls, people started to wander about the deck. Some wandered forward to the prow, where the men argued about who was brave enough to descend into the forecastle. Others stared down into the open hold, which had eight feet of water and a three-foot sea turtle swimming in it.

"Strange horse," said Onderdonk the Very Tall Woodcutter.

"Strange horse," agreed Kareesha Kawasaki.

"Odd saddle," Onderdonk said, indicating the shell.

"Hard saddle," said Kareesha Kawasaki.

Alone at the stern, Emmaline ascended a ladder to the poop deck and idly pushed the tiller. It swung loose, clicking in its chocks like chattering teeth.

"Emmaline!" she heard a whisper. *"Psst!"*

.Flurp was motioning to her from a hatch he had opened. Emmaline joined him and peered into it. She saw a ladder leading down into a dark, flooded passageway.

"Should we?" Flurp said.

Emmaline hesitated. Sometimes, Emmaline had bad dreams in which she found herself plunged up to her neck in swift-flowing dark waters, sinking below the surface and crying out helplessly to be saved.

"Emmaline! Where are you?" It was her mother's

voice, coming from the prow of the ship.

Quick as thought, before her mother could spot her, the girl scurried into the open hatch and scrambled down the ladder, plunging up to her knees in smelly, turbid water. In a moment, Flurp joined her. Around them floated bits of wood, pieces of clothing, a boot, and other flotsam. Something brushed Emmaline's leg, and when she plucked it out of the water, she found it was a painted portrait in a gold frame, oval and about as big as her hand, of a beautiful dark-haired young woman in a white dress. She studied the picture, liked it, and stuck it in her belt. Then she and Flurp moved out of the light from the open hatch and waded down the dim passage into deeper water. Soon it had almost reached their waists. Fishes' fins and mouths tickled Emmaline's calves.

They passed several open doorways. Looking through one, Emmaline vaguely made out a ruined storeroom; through another, a cabin with two beds.

"I wish we'd brought a candle," Flurp said behind her. "It's dark. Shadowy. Dismal. Gloomy. Tenebrous."

"*Shhh!*" Emmaline said, holding up a hand. "I think I heard something!"

They moved ahead quietly. At the end of the passageway, they came to a bright red door that was closed—not only closed but locked, latched on this side, as if someone had wanted to keep prisoner whoever or whatever was inside. Emmaline's eyes had adjusted to the dark by now and she could make out Flurp looking at her as if he was asking what they should do.

"I'm sure I heard something," Emmaline whispered.

"I don't hear anything," he whispered back.

They listened again in silence. The sound of their breath in this small space seemed very loud. Then, from far away, the girl heard her mother's voice outside. Her mother's footsteps approached down the deck overhead.

"Where are you, Emmaline?" her mother's voice called.

Emmaline threw the latch and pushed the red door open against the resistance of the water. The disturbed water rose, then settled back. At first, there was nothing to see, just a great gaping dark hole before them. Then, dimly, Emmaline made out a small cabin.

"Come on, Em," Flurp said nervously. He touched her elbow. "There's nothing in there. Let's go."

Suddenly, something moved inside the cabin, and Emmaline screamed.

7

They Meet the Enemy

At the sound of Emmaline's scream, galloping footsteps thundered across the deck overhead and voices called out, "Where are you? Where are you?"

"We're down here!" Emmaline yelled upward.

Flurp shouted, "Bring some light!"

Emmaline could hear her mother screaming her name up above, outside the hatch. *Emmaline, Emmaline, where are you? . . .*

"I'm all right, Mother!" the girl called. "I'm fine!"

The dim passageway grew even dimmer for a moment as several people dropped through the hatch at its far end. Figures splashed toward them down the dark passageway.

"All be well now, children," Minister Moonster

said with a quivering voice as he approached. "Fear not. Fear not." The minister was followed by Bob the Milkmaid, Miss Darkniss the Candle Maker, and Luigi the Carpenter's Husband.

"Be careful!" Flurp said. "There's somebody down here."

Miss Darkniss always wore a string of her wares around her neck, and now she detached a beeswax taper. Bob the Milkmaid struck a flint to light it. A blue spark shot out, the wick caught flame, and the dim passage grew brighter and brighter with a flickering orange glow. The light soon reached Emmaline and Flurp near the closed door. Emmaline had been quick enough to pull the door shut and relatch it.

She now pointed to the red door and said, "In there."

Minister Moonster whispered to the others, "Keep your weapons ready, but use no violence. Unless," he added as an afterthought, "it be absolutely necessary, of course. If I die in this effort, bury me under the apple tree." Then he added, "The second apple tree, not the first apple tree." Then he added, "The one with the crooked trunk, by the chapel wall."

The minister's fingers moved toward the latch, and the others raised their various weapons. The minister breathed a prayer, threw the latch, and shoved the door open. A rank, stale odor wafted out.

"Come out of there immediately, please!" the minister yelled.

Nothing happened.

Miss Darkniss raised the candle and moved it through the doorway. Emmaline's whole body pounded like a heart as she peered around the door frame. Some empty shelves on a wall flickered into view, then the far corner of a low ceiling, then a darker form, hunched up on a cot, someone staring at them without moving.

He was very small—as small as a child. Completely naked, his body was covered with thick brown hair. He had intense, darkly luminous eyes and a long, protruding jaw with large teeth.

"Eek," he said very quietly. *"Eek eek!"*

Here is a picture of him:

"*Eek,*" he said again.

"So that's what a Frenchman looks like!" whispered Bob the Milkmaid.

"We mean no harm, sir," Minister Moonster said with a quivering voice. "Put down your weapons instantly!"

"He has no weapons," pointed out Luigi the Carpenter's Husband.

"He may have invisible French weapons" was the rejoinder.

"*Eek,*" the Frenchman whispered, still without moving.

"I think he's sick," Emmaline said, and impulsively waded into the cabin.

"Emmaline, stop!" Flurp called, but the girl kept going till she stopped at the edge of the bed.

"Hel-lo," she said, speaking slowly and distinctly to make the foreigner understand. "Wel-come to Mac-Oonga-foond-sen. My name—is—Emmaline—Perth. That's Emma-*line*, not Emma-*leen*."

She held out a hand to shake in friendly fashion. The Frenchman eeked and weakly touched her hand with a single wrinkled finger.

"He *is* sick!" she cried. "Flurp, will you carry him out?"

The others instantly agreed that Young Flurp was just the person for the job and pushed him forward.

Moments later, on deck, Flurp came up through the hatch with the hairy little Frenchman cradled in his arms. When the crowd on board saw the stranger, a cry of horror went up.

"It's the French!" Mrs. Overbite exclaimed, and fell into her husband's arms, staggering him backward and nearly knocking him down.

"Emmaline!" Jane Perth called out. She rushed

forward to upbraid her daughter for going into the ship.

"I'm all *right,* Mother," Emmaline kept repeating. "I'm all *right.* Really."

Flurp laid the foreigner down on the deck. Everybody made a circle around him, several paces back.

"*Eek,*" the little fellow said, looking from face to face.

"It's a Frenchman all right," sneered Shmink the Bailiff. He had been cowering behind a mast all this time. "I recognize the lingo. And this is a brutal killer, too, by his looks. Ugh! How he stinks!"

"Speak for yourself, Mr. Shmink," muttered Emmaline.

"What do we do about him?" asked Bob the Milkmaid.

"Or with him," said somebody else.

"*To* him, is more like it," said Shmink, who now took a cautious step forward. "What is thy name, sir?" he demanded.

"*Eek!*"

"Well, Mr. *Eek,* I am Lexter Shmink the Bailiff of MacOongafoondsen, and I arrest thee as a foreign spy and a thief." Shmink whipped the blank scroll from his pocket, flipped it open, and held the parchment an inch from his face, as if actually reading from it. "I hereby take you into custody according to MacOongafoondsen City Statute . . . ummm"—he paused while he made up a number—"one four seven six three. Spying and theft are capital charges. Therefore, until your trial, you will be held in the city jail."

"We have no city jail," Luigi the Carpenter's Husband reminded him.

"I was *trying* to *scare* him," Shmink growled under his breath.

"Sorry."

"You will be held until your trial in my dank and rat-filled cellar," the bailiff continued, correcting himself. "You will be treated humanely, given a fair trial, found guilty, and shot until you are dead."

"We have no guns in MacOongafoondsen," Luigi the Carpenter's Husband reminded him.

"You will be hanged by the neck until you are dead," amended Shmink.

"Wait just one minute," a voice protested.

8

Justice Aboard the Justice

It was Emmaline who had spoken, and she now stepped forward.

"How do you know he's a spy?" she demanded.

"He's a Frenchman," said Shmink. "Are the French our enemies? They are. Do enemies spy on their enemies? They do. Therefore, he's been spying. Therefore, he's a spy."

"How do you know he's a thief?"

"Have there not been thefts of late? There have been. Are any of us thieves? We are not. Therefore, this person must be the thief. Process of elimination. He may even have the goose, the cup, and the sweater hidden on his person right now," Shmink said, though the Frenchman quite clearly had nowhere to hide anything.

"The goose and the cup and the sweater disappeared six days ago," Emmaline argued. "This man just got here."

"We don't know that," Shmink the Bailiff put in. "Nobody in MacOongafoondsen ever goes to the sea because we are rightly and traditionally fearful of the sea. We only know that Young Flurp the Town Fool discovered the ship this morning. This ship could've been sitting here for months! Years!"

"How could this man have survived without food or freshwater, locked in his cabin?" Emmaline asked sardonically.

"Well . . . " The bailiff thought about that a moment. "Maybe he locked it himself, when he heard us coming."

"From the *outside*?" Emmaline snickered.

"He must be a brave man," said Peaches Cobbler, "to sail this big boat here all by himself."

"The French," her husband observed, "they are a hairy race."

"Short, too," said Onderdonk the Very Tall Woodcutter, who was just under four feet four himself.

"*I* find him handsome," smiled Ongka the Fat Bread Maker, adjusting her bodice more alluringly and smoothing her hair.

"None of that, now, none of that," grumbled Hammerklavver the Blacksmith.

"He looks wicked to me," said one of the Grogniks.

"I see no harm about him," countered his twin brother.

"They be a lewd and pagan race," observed Minister Moonster, "to walk about naked as monkeys."

"*Eek,*" the Frenchman said.

"Small vocabulary," Flurp noted. "Few words. Limited language. *Pocas palabras.*"

"Obviously," Shmink said, taking control of the situation again, "he's been instructed to tell us nothing but his name. It's an old enemy spy trick."

Emmaline said, "I *think* he's asking for water."

"He's been in plenty of water," Shmink snapped.

"Salt water," the girl snapped back. "He needs freshwater. And food."

"What do Frenchmen eat?" queried Kareesha Kawasaki.

"French fries," said Miss Darkniss the Candle Maker. "French toast. French dressing. French dip. And French vanilla ice cream."

Bob the Milkmaid handed Emmaline a goatskin bottle full of water. The girl knelt with it beside the Frenchman.

"Be wary," warned the bailiff. "He may rip thy throat out."

"Drink, monsieur," she said.

"So his first name is *M'sew,* eh," sneered Shmink.

"*Monsieur* is French for 'mister,'" Emmaline said.

"I knew that," countered the bailiff. "I was testing you."

Emmaline eased the goatskin between the Frenchman's lips and poured. He sipped hungrily, his eyes glowing with gratitude.

"There's a tag around his neck," Emmaline said, and read what was stamped on the tin medal. "It says 'Samuel.'"

By now, Mr. Overbite had freed himself from his wife.

"What news, Mr. Shmink?" he demanded.

"Sir!" Shmink saluted off the dead sparrow on his hat brim. "We have apprehended one Samuel Eek, a Frenchman who as good as confessed to being a spy and a thief."

"He did not!" Emmaline cried.

"I invoke City Statute one four seven six three," Shmink said. "Take him away!"

"Just one minute!" Emmaline's voice was heard again. "I've never heard of City Statute one four seven six three. Where is that listed?"

"Where is it *listed*?" sputtered Shmink. "It's listed right here," he said, whipping the blank scroll and flashing it quickly, as if everybody there didn't know it was blank. "In very, very small print."

Emmaline said, "What about City Statute fifty-three? Which is in my father's law book in very *large* print, if you'd like to read it."

"City Statute fifty-three? . . ." said Shmink, who'd never heard of it. "Remind your fellow citizens of its gist."

"City Statute fifty-three says that if there's no

evidence, a suspect may be released into the custody of his or her lawyer."

"His *lawyer?*" exclaimed Mayor Overbite. "Who is this Frenchman's lawyer?"

"I am," said Emmaline Perth.

9

Conspiracy at Midnight

The citizens returned to town in small, animated groups, with Monsieur Eek in Flurp's arms and his attorney, Emmaline Perth, walking alongside. The mayor had had no choice but to release the Frenchman into Emmaline's custody.

"I don't like this, Emmaline," her mother said on the way. "I don't like it at all."

Emmaline stopped in her tracks and looked in her mother's face. "What do you think Father would have done?" she demanded.

Her mother's eyes dropped and she said nothing. Both of them knew that Gabriel Perth would have done exactly what his daughter was doing right now. Any sign of injustice or cruelty had always roused that gentle man to a fury.

The other citizens were all achatter about the events of the morning—not only the arrival of the first ship ever, and of the first foreigner, but an arrest on capital charges and an impending trial. Everyone agreed that this would be the Trial of the Century in MacOongafoondsen—simply because it was the *only* trial in a century at least.

"What means a capital charge, Mr. Shmink?" asked Hammerklavver the Blacksmith.

"A capital charge, Hammerklavver the Blacksmith?" The bailiff stalled while he tried to think up a definition.

"Technical, I mean," said Hammerklavver.

"*Technically,*" the bailiff lied, "a capital charge means that it's capital—which is to say, wonderful—that the criminal in question has been charged."

"No, it doesn't," Emmaline interrupted. She had overheard this exchange. "*Capital* comes from *caput,* which is Latin for 'head.' A capital charge means you can lose your head. It means you can be executed."

"No need to lose *your* head, young lady," the bailiff joked feebly, then whispered to

Hammerklavver, "Ruined by her father. Too many books."

Emmaline saw some of her mother's old fire, and her mother's own strong sense of justice, when they stood before their shop once more and Mr. Overbite decided to assert his authority again.

"*Mazoor* Eek," the mayor said pompously, "I hereby order you to stay within this house until you are brought to trial. And Mrs. Perth, I hereby order you—"

"You may order me nothing, Ignoratius Overbite," Jane Perth rapped out. "Do you think I don't know my rights and duties? Do I not pay my civil taxes each April fifteenth? Do I not vote? And don't think I ever voted for *you*. I will act according to my conscience and the law, and when you think I've broken the law, you may arrest me, too. Come, Emmaline. Come, Young Flurp. Come, sir," she said to Monsieur Eek.

With that, she went inside and slammed the door shut in the mayor's face, leaving the man protesting aloud with a sound like "*Buhh—buhh—buhh. . . .*"

Shmink the Bailiff blew a few notes on his official tin trumpet.

"Clear the streets! Everybody disperse! Akmed the Cobbler, have you no shoes to cobble? Onderdonk the Very Tall Woodcutter, have you no very tall wood to cut? Everybody about his business!"

The citizens moved off, but no shoes got cobbled and no tall wood got shorter and no business got transacted that day. All MacOonga-foondsen was abuzz.

That same night, in the very middle of the night, a low figure scuttled from shadow to shadow, slinking like a ferret up Only Street, swaddled up to the eyes in an inky cloak, a hat pulled low. When the figure reached the back door of the mayor's house, he let out a low whistle and the door opened to admit him, then shut noiselessly.

"Well met, Mr. Shm—" the mayor began, just inside the door.

The bailiff held up a hand, stopping him. "No names, sir," he said. "Please. If no *names* are exchanged, you might say two people never met, mightn't you?"

"Legally correct, my careful friend. Legally correct." The mayor knew the law when the law served his purposes.

Shmink had entered a well-sealed chamber at the back of the mayor's house. The thick, plush curtains of the room were pulled tightly shut. A low, smoky fire in the hearth fouled the air. The mayor seated himself in a thronelike chair behind a desk.

"Now," he said, "to the business. And the business, in short, is that *I don't like* this Frenchman." As he spoke, he took up a parchment from his desk and twisted it slowly between his fat fingers. A gold ring, several sizes too small, had swelled one finger to the thickness of a bratwurst. "Why don't I like him? I don't know. Maybe because he's French. But I'll say it again: *I do not like the Frenchman.*"

"Maybe to be safe," Shmink suggested, "we should refer to . . . the individual in question as 'Monsieur X.'"

"Ah, yes. Good idea. Monsieur X."

"Let the *X* stand for Executed."

The two men laughed grimly, like accomplices.

"I say this Monsieur X is a civic danger," pronounced the mayor. "He's a public enemy."

"And a fop," added the ill-dressed Shmink.

"No foreigner is going to make a baboon out of me."

"No, sir."

"What a silly name, too. *Eek*," sneered Ignoratius Overbite.

"An idiotic moniker," agreed Lexter Shmink.

"I want this Monsieur X convicted."

"As do I, sir."

"I want him"—the mayor was about to say one word, then changed it—"gone."

"As do I, sir."

"Permanently gone."

"Understood, sir."

"By any means possible." The mayor's fingers wrung the parchment like a throat.

"Then we may need to—how shall I put it?— *convince the populace*," Shmink suggested. "We may need to nurture a guilty verdict. Plant it and water it and fertilize it, so to speak."

"Fertilizer," said the mayor. "Excellent idea."

"And may I remind you you're up for reelection soon?"

"Very true."

"Nothing like a little fear to get the populace behind you. A successful trial might help your campaign, which, truth to tell, is a bit shaky since you raised taxes four hundred percent."

"Is the population fully behind us, firmly behind us, or partly behind us?"

"Mostly behind us, sir."

"We must get them totally behind us, Mr. Shm—"

"No names, sir."

"No names. Indeed."

"And we never met here tonight."

"We never met at all, anywhere, anytime. Is there any other business?"

"I believe that's all, sir."

"To bed, then. Good-night, Mr. Shmink."

"Good-night, Mr. Mayor."

The door opened onto darkness, and Mr. Shmink went out, blending into the night.

As the door shut, the plush curtains parted as

if by themselves and Lucretia Overbite stepped forward.

"Well done, my dear," she said, patting the mayor's cheek. "Very well done."

The town slept. Injustice, as always, lay waking.

10

Medicine

On arriving in the Perth house, Monsieur Eek was so weak, he simply lay on his bed in a near coma for a day. Emmaline spoon-fed him lukewarm broths to strengthen him, gradually adding nuts and apples and pears from the winter hoard in the cellar. Mrs. Perth started giving him the remains of their dinners, though she would not allow Monsieur Eek to eat at the downstairs table with them. She insisted he had to eat in his room.

Monsieur Eek had suffered some deep cuts from being thrown around his cabin during the storm, so Emmaline took down her father's old medicine cabinet, a wooden chest about a yard high that unlatched and opened like a book. Its shelves were stocked with crystal vials containing red and green and blue liquids and powders and potions, each marked with a label in her father's small, neat hand. YEW TREE BARK, FOR FEVER. WILLOW DUST, AGAINST MEGRIMS. SAINT JOHN'S WEED, EXCELLENT AGAINST MELANCHOLY. She consulted his yellowed handwritten notes and found how to mix healing lotions and salves.

One day while she bound a poultice on a wound, Emmaline questioned her guest about his life and travels.

"You've seen the world, Monsieur Eek. What's it like?"

"Eek."

"Beautiful?"

"Eek eek."

"Very beautiful?"

"Eek."

"What about France?"

"Eek."

"Lush green valleys? Snowcapped mountains?"

"Eek."

"And deep dark forests? . . ."

"Eek! Eek eek!"

"Cities, too?"

"Eek."

"Great cities? What about the city you came from?"

"Eek."

"How many people does it have? A hundred?"

"Eek eek."

"A thousand? A whole thousand people in one place?"

"Eek!"

"And I'll bet a river runs through it."

"Eek eek."

"Ten stone bridges? That many? And I'll bet you can stroll through the town and pass people you don't even know."

"Eek."

"It's one of your favorite things to do?"

"Eek."

"Yes, I'd love it, too. Well, Samuel . . . may I call you Samuel?"

"Eek!"

"You may stop calling me Miss Perth and call me Emmaline."

"Eek eek."

"Emma-*line,* not Emma-*leen.*"

"Eek."

"Thank you. Well, Samuel, I'd love to see your country someday. That is," she added more soberly, "after your trial. . . ."

That was the day Emmaline started preparing her case.

At first, Jane Perth came only as far as the door of Monsieur Eek's room. Gradually, she edged her way in and would sit and watch him with Emmaline. But on one point, she remained adamant: She refused to let the Frenchman eat with them at the downstairs table.

"But Mother," Emmaline protested, "if we don't let Samuel eat with us, it means we don't think he's our equal. After all, he *is* a human being."

Monsieur Eek grabbed a shiny pewter goblet out of Jane Perth's hands and bit its edge. The woman grabbed the goblet back.

"I will not let him sit at my table," she insisted. "And now that he's up and about, will you please ask him to stop *taking* things?"

Monsieur Eek was not only up and about these days; he was all over the walls and ceiling and back and forth over cabinets and hopping over their heads, running up and down the staircase and exploring the house, often making off along the way with a brooch or a spoon or a candlesnuffer or anything else that glinted and caught his eye.

"What curious habits the French have," Emmaline said to Flurp one afternoon when he dropped by for a reading lesson. "This morning, I found him hanging upside down from the attic rafters."

"I do that sometimes," Flurp admitted, looking somewhat sheepish.

"Do you somersault down the stairs and do back flips?"

"No," said Flurp, "that would be a little too strange."

Just then, the Frenchman leapt into Emmaline's lap, chattered at Flurp in his curious tongue, grabbed the rainbow cap off the young man's head, and dashed away, running sideways around the walls with it.

"Maybe it's culture shock," Flurp suggested.

"Eek eek eek eek!"

"What did he say?" Flurp asked.

"I don't really know," the girl admitted. "I'm not making much progress in French."

She certainly had been trying hard enough. Every morning, she would sit Monsieur Eek down for a language lesson and would try to get him to say, "Not guilty, Your Honor"—so far, without any success.

"I do speak a few words," she told Flurp.

"Tell me some. I'd love to learn some French words."

"*Eek!*" the girl said. "*Eek eek eek!*"

"*Eek! Eek eek eek!*" Flurp repeated. "What does that mean?"

"Well," Emmaline had to admit, "I don't really know."

Monsieur Eek landed in her lap again and chattered at the girl. She chattered back at him. "*Eek eek eek eek eek.*"

"You two seem to be chatting very well," Flurp said.

Monsieur Eek planted a kiss on Emmaline's cheek and wrapped his hairy arms around her neck. At this, Flurp looked troubled.

"Emmaline," he said, "I hope . . . I mean . . ."

"You hope what, Flurp?"

"I hope we'll always stay good friends. I know

Monsieur has a lot of Gallic charm. He's very suave and elegant and cosmopolitan and all that. . . ."

Emmaline just laughed.

"Flurp, if we ever stop being best friends, I'll *strangle* you!"

Flurp did not laugh along with her.

"You're a lawyer now," he said. "Or practically so. I'm still just Young Flurp the Town Fool. And I've got these . . . these blue eyes," he added bitterly.

"You're only Flurp the Town Fool," his friend said, "because you *let* people call you the town fool. And you let people act toward you as if you *were* the town fool. Just because your father was town fool doesn't mean you have to be. Change professions. Call yourself Flurp the Town Crier. You cried the news about the ship the day you found it."

"Eek," said Monsieur Eek.

"Monsieur Eek agrees. And frankly, Flurp, I *like* your blue eyes."

Flurp looked relieved, and her guest leapt off the girl's lap and went back to running around the walls.

"The French sure are energetic," Flurp observed. "Spirited. Lively. Vimful, vigorous, and vital."

"And there are people in this town who don't like Monsieur Eek," Emmaline mused, "just because he's French!"

She was interrupted by the harsh clang of a bell in the street.

"A proclamation from the mayor!" cried the voice of Lexter Shmink.

The war for the hearts and minds of Mac-Oongafoondsen was about to begin.

11

A Town Divided

Shmink was standing on the edge of the town well, ringing the town bell.

"Eerie, eerie!" he wailed as a crowd gathered. "Eerie, eerie" was Shmink's twisted, misunderstood version of "Hear ye, hear ye!" As Emmaline and Flurp came up to the edge of the crowd, Shmink unrolled his blank scroll as if to read an official proclamation.

"The scroll is upside down!" Emmaline couldn't resist calling out, and Shmink quickly reversed it.

"By order of Ignoratius B. Overbite, the mayor of the great coastal city of Mac—"

"Cut to the meat course!" called Onderdonk the Very Tall Woodcutter.

"Silence!" screamed Shmink. Then he ran his finger over invisible print to find his place, and

continued. "To show our support for the great coastal city of . . . et cetera . . . against *foreign forces* . . ."

He paused there, emphasizing the words and casting a meaningful look around the crowd.

". . . against *foreign forces,* be they *French* or any other kind, let all citizens fly the black-and-gold flag!"

There was a silence. Everyone stared at him.

"What black-and-gold flag?" called Miss Darkniss.

"The black-and-gold flag of MacOonga-foondsen. This great city's colors being"—the bailiff paused again for a moment—"black and gold lamé."

Luigi the Carpenter's Husband said, "I didn't know black and gold lamé were the city's colors."

"Well they are now," Shmink snapped, "so fly them. All hail the black and gold lamé flag!"

In fact, black and gold had only been the town's colors since that morning, when Mrs. Overbite suggested them because she happened to look good in black and gold lamé.

"Black-and-gold stars, or black-and-gold

stripes?" asked Kareesha Kawasaki.

Shmink stared at her blankly for a moment.

"Both," he finally said.

Bob the Milkmaid said, "Horizontal stripes, or vertical stripes?"

"Both," said Shmink again, improvising wildly.

"How many stars?" asked Hammerklavver.

"Black on the left, or gold on the left?" asked Peaches Cobbler.

"Are there any diamonds or trapezoids in the pattern?" someone called.

"Silence!" shrieked Shmink. His face had flushed and swollen to the color and consistency of an over-ripe tomato. "Just fly thee a flag and make sure it's black and gold! And make sure you join our city's sports team, too!"

There was another silence.

"What sports team?" someone said.

"The *team,* the city *sports* team," the bailiff sputtered. "The MacOongafoondsen . . . Ostriches."

"What's an ostrich?" somebody called.

"Never mind! It's the city bird."

"What game do the Ostriches play?" called out Kawasaki the Left-Handed Farmer.

Everyone waited in silence a moment.

"Badminton," said Shmink.

Flurp had been getting more and more agitated during all this, and now he burst out. "You can't make me fly a flag!" he said. "Black and gold or anything else! And you can't *order* me to play badminton! I'll play badminton on my own time, without you and without ostriches!"

"Ah-*ha*!" cried Shmink. "So thou art a traitor to thy city, eh, Young Flurp?"

"Because of *badminton*?"

"Because you refuse to show your support for our great city."

"I won't fly no flag, neither," muttered one of the Grognik twins. "Especially no black and gold lamé one!"

"Well, *I* will," the other twin shot back at him.

"I see nothing wrong with this Frenchman," said Kareesha Kawasaki.

"Well, *I* do," her husband countered. "He's not from here and let him go back to wherever he came from!"

"I think this smooth little Frenchie be come here to steal our women," Hammerklavver the

Blacksmith growled out. He could not forget that his sweetheart, Ongka, actually found this brute handsome.

"He aren't all that smooth," said Barbara the Carpenter, pulling a wood chip from her teeth. "His body be more hairyful than the top of my head."

"I say he be disgusting," spat Hammerklavver, who was nearly as hairy as Monsieur Eek himself and could go about without a shirt in winter because he had a back like a mink.

"I do love gold lamé," Fierfl the Tailor put in quietly. He foresaw a booming new business making flags.

"I don't like badminton," grumbled Luigi.

"Ah-ha!" cried Shmink. "Another traitor!"

"Since when does the mayor tell us what we can and can't do?" asked Miss Darkniss of everyone around her.

"More traitors!" exulted Shmink.

In a moment, voices were raised on all sides, arguing for and against a flag, for and against badminton, for and against Monsieur Eek. The clanging of the town bell stopped them all.

"The trial of Samuel Eek," Shmink announced,

"will take place in three days by order of His Honor, Mayor Ignoratius B. Overbite! Be you all present— and *show where your loyalties lie.* Now disperse instantly! Patriots and traitors—all of you!"

He watched now as the twenty-one citizens of MacOongafoondsen headed home arguing, in groups. Then he quickly found his way up Only Street to the mayor's house. The mayor himself opened the door with a fur-trimmed dinner napkin around his throat.

Shmink displayed his curdled teeth in a grin.

"Worked like a charm," he said.

By the next morning, the town had split into factions for and against the Frenchman. The pro-Eek faction gathered at Miss Darkniss the Candle Maker's and wore armbands of pastel pink-and-green dots, matching the flag found on the ship; the anti-Eeks met in front of Fierfl the Tailor's shop and wore armbands of black and gold lamé. There was no room to gather inside Fierfl's shop because his tailoring family had been collecting loose thread for centuries, and all those threads, tied end to end, now made up a multicolored ball that stood eight feet high at the back of the shop, forcing Fierfl into a corner up front.

Whole families divided over Eek. Kareesha Kawasaki was pro-Eek, her husband anti. Barbara the Carpenter was anti-Eek; Luigi, her husband, was pro. Tom and Tim Grognik the Twin Tavern Keepers split on the subject, which made evenings at the tavern difficult for both factions, because you couldn't tell if the Grognik who was serving you was Tim or Tom, pro or anti. Soon the pro-Eekers took the tavern tables to the left, by the spicy buffalo turkey wings, while anti-Eekers took the tables to the right, near the batter-fried goose wings, thus giving birth to the terms *left-wingers* and *right-wingers*. Tim and Tom Grognik could be heard yelling accusations at each other in the kitchen.

"Toady!"

"Traitor!"

"Conformist!"

"Collaborator!"

Then the brothers stopped talking to each other entirely, which meant no more of their famous pickled samphire and tansy pie, or any kind of wings. One day, the brothers appeared sporting four matching black eyes, and everyone knew why.

Signs and banners and bumper stickers on horse carts started appearing, saying things like EEK OUT! and WE LIKE EEK! EEK'S A SNEAK! EEK'S THE PEAK! EEK REEKS! EEK'S A GEEK! EEK'S UNIQUE! BEWARE OF EEK-BEARING SHIPS! JOIN THE EEK CLIQUE! and SAMUEL SHMAMUEL! Citizens with opposing bumper stickers glared at one another now from their carts as they sat at the WHOA! sign on Only Street.

Meanwhile, the newly formed MacOonga-foondsen Ostriches were out every morning in their black shorts and gold lamé jerseys, playing badminton and cheering themselves on alone. Since the Ostriches were the only team in town and all the members played on the same side of the net, their games tended to be short and simple: The Ostriches would declare victory, high-five each other, sing a song, and go home.

Now only one day remained until the trial of Samuel Eek. Barbara the Carpenter gathered lumber for a gallows.

12

Law

It was the middle of the night, and again a lone candle burned in all the town, behind the shutters of the tumbledown shop at the far end of Only Street. Again, Emmaline Perth sat over her father's law books—but now she studied them in deadly earnest. Propped in front of her sat the small portrait Emmaline had found in the ship. Salt water had warped the wooden oval and cracked the portrait's surface, but the beauty of the young woman in the painting was undiminished. Her calm, level gaze looked out at Emmaline as if to give her patience and hope. At first, Emmaline thought this might be Monsieur Eek's wife, but his only reaction when she showed him the portrait was to try to bite it.

Now Emmaline looked up from her page to the picture and gasped a little. Had the young woman in white really just blinked her long lashes and smiled at her? . . .

Emmaline jerked awake in her chair. She had been dozing off. She rose and stepped out the front door of the shop to let the night air reawaken her.

A light, salty spring wind was blowing down Only Street from the Great Northern Ocean. A half-moon was up, with stars spilled around it like silver coins on black velvet. The metallic stars practically clinked. No lights shone in any of the city's houses. The night lay so still she could hear the bare branches of the dead birch trees rattling below Old Castle Rock. Vaguely, Emmaline wondered if the crimson ghost of Angus MacOongafoondsen was walking the castle halls tonight. Now as she looked up to Old Castle Rock, she could swear she saw a shadow stealing up the hillside among the other shadows, a figure climbing toward the ruined fortress. . . .

"*Who?*" asked the owl in the marsh. "*Who's who?*"

Then the figure was gone. Emmaline shivered. Probably just her imagination.

She started strolling up Only Street against the

breeze. In a moment, she had passed the town well. The wind in the well's throat made a deep, wavering moan. Before Emmaline knew it, she was past the mayor's house (as always, she avoided looking at it); then she had left the town behind and was standing at the bottom of Edge of the Sea Hill. In the moonlight, the spears of grass on the hillside gleamed like miniature knives, yet the knives only rustled harmlessly around her ankles as she ascended. She felt weightless and refreshed. The sky grew and grew all the way up; then as she crested the top and the void of the sea boomed before her, she seemed to be flying through the universe. She looked down the side of the cliff and felt a shock and a pang of loss.

The ship was gone. The beach was empty. Suddenly dizzy, Emmaline swayed on the edge of the precipice, about to fall. . . .

"Emmaline! Emmaline, wake up!"

It was her mother, shaking her shoulder.

"Not guilty, Your Honor!" the girl said, waking and sitting up. Then she said, "What is it? . . ."

"You fell asleep."

Emmaline looked around and realized she was

still in the shop. Her candle had burned down to nothing, and dawn was glazing the window. The law book that had become her pillow sat open on the table before her.

"The ship is gone," she muttered.

"What, darling?"

"The ship is gone! Monsieur Eek has left!"

She started out of her chair, but her mother gently held her back.

"The ship is on the beach and Monsieur Eek is asleep in his bed. I just saw him."

Then Emmaline remembered something else with another shock. This time it was real.

"The trial is today," she said. "I'm not prepared!"

She frantically started leafing through the book before her, reaching for her quill. Her mother took the pen out of her hand.

"My daughter," she said, "you've done enough. Go to your bed and rest. I'll wake you in time for court."

"But Mother . . ."

"You know enough. What you need now is sleep."

Emmaline moved limp as a sleepwalker in her

mother's arms. Upstairs, Emmaline began to un-
dress, but her mother finished for her, then eased
the girl onto the creaking horsehair mattress, pulled
the blanket up, and brushed the long brown bangs
out of her daughter's closing eyes.

Next thing Emmaline knew, she was sitting up
in her bed and being blinded by morning light. Her
mother was calling her down to breakfast. Clothes
for the day were all laid out for her—but there was
one garment among the clothes that she didn't
recognize at first. Then she realized it was her father's
black law robe. Her mother had rehemmed and
resewn it to fit her. On the robe lay Gabriel Perth's
curled white courtroom wig, and a note in her
mother's hand: "So that your father will be with you
today."

Emmaline rushed downstairs to thank her
mother and found another surprise: Monsieur Eek
was sitting at the family table in a chair opposite her
own. Her mother stood cooking at the fireplace, as
if there was nothing odd about this foreigner sitting
at their table.

"Mother," Emmaline said, embracing her, "you
are spec-*tac*-ular."

Jane Perth smiled and returned the embrace; then she and her daughter sat down together at table.

"Monsieur Eek," Jane said, "will you please say grace?"

The Frenchman put his hands together as he had seen them do, then said, *"Eek!"*

"Amen," said Jane and Emmaline Perth.

13

MacOongafoondsen Versus Eek

MacOongafoondsen had no courthouse, so the town chapel served as courtroom instead. Minister Moonster stood in front of the chapel now, banging the Ancient Iron Spoon of Law on the Great Frying Pan of Justice to announce a trial and summon the people. This was ancient MacOongafoondsen tradition. The minister hardly needed to bang the Great Frying Pan of Justice, since everyone in town was already in the courtroom except Shmink the Bailiff, who today was Shmink the Prosecuting Attorney.

Attention was all on Monsieur Eek, who was sitting next to Emmaline at the defense table—or rather, *on* the defense table. For the trial, Jane Perth had made him a dignified royal blue jacket with frogged buttons and lace cuffs in the French style, though the Frenchman remained, as he preferred, barefoot.

Twenty minutes late, the bailiff swept up the chapel aisle, took a position at the front of the courtroom, and proclaimed, "Eerie, eerie, eerie! Court is now convened for the case of the *Great Coastal City of MacOongafoondsen versus the Base Vile Frenchman M'sewer Samuel Eek!* All rise to be sworn in as jury!"

By ancient custom, the entire citizenry of MacOongafoondsen served as jury in criminal cases. They rose now from their benches but did not hold up their hands; instead, following MacOongafoondsen tradition, they solemnly pointed their left pinkies at their foreheads. This was how the people of MacOongafoondsen had always taken their oaths.

Shmink said, "Do you swear to hear the evidence and give a fair and honest verdict?"

"We do," everyone said, twitching their pinkies once.

Secretly, Shmink winked to several people in the courtroom—to Fierfl the Tailor and Hammer-klavver the Blacksmith and Barbara the Carpenter and others who were already set against Monsieur Eek and prepared to vote guilty. Emmaline noticed Shmink's wink and felt a bristle of panic up the back of her neck.

"All sit," commanded Shmink, and they sat. Then he said, "All rise!" and they rose again.

Mayor Overbite marched in, wearing a black and gold lamé judge's robe with a large *M* on the back and a white curled wig. The wig was more dingy gray than white, and the severe curls had loosened into dangling hair sausages. Moths had eaten a hole in the side. The wig was also far too small for the mayor's fat head, and sat perched on his shiny bald pate like a dishrag on a muskmelon. Every few seconds, the wig would slide to one side or skitter forward and Mr. Overbite would smack the peruke against his head to keep it from falling off altogether. The wig would exhale a cloud of ancient yellow dust and he would sneeze.

"Be seated," he pronounced pompously, and sneezed. Then, seating himself behind the table that served as his judicial bench, he banged his gavel and its wooden head flew off. *"Bang,"* he said, speaking for the gavel. The citizens of Mac-Oongafoondsen ducked as the gavel's head flew by, then sat down.

"Silence in the courtroom!" shrieked Shmink, though no one was talking.

"I see the defendant wishes to flout our local customs," Judge Overbite observed. Monsieur Eek was doing head rolls on the defendant's table.

"Get down, Samuel," Emmaline whispered. "You have to make a good impression."

"Read the charges, Mr. Prosecutor," the judge commanded.

Shmink whipped the blank scroll from his pocket and pressed it to his eye.

"Samuel Eek, thou art accused of stealing one fat goose, roasted. . . ."

"That were our goose," whispered Peaches Cobbler.

"One red sweater with a spot of fried egg on the front. . . ."

"That were my sweater," whispered Bob the Milkmaid.

"And one cup, golden and bejeweled with rubies and amethysts and emeralds and turquoise."

"That were the chapel's chalice," said Minister Moonster the Minister, "and cursèd be the base villain who took it."

The bailiff turned over the blank scroll as if there were something written on the other side.

"Thou also standest accused of spying for France. As evidence, I submit this French flag." Shmink laid the wrinkled pink-and-green-dotted flag on the judge's bench. "How dost thou plead, Samuel Eek?"

Emmaline prodded Monsieur Eek, who again jumped onto the table.

"Eek," he said.

"Not guilty," Emmaline translated.

"Not guilty, eh," sneered Judge Overbite. His wig skied down his forehead and he managed to grab it just over his nose, squeezing a puff of dust from it like pollen from a sunflower. He sneezed. "Well, sir," he said, "you will receive a fair trial in *our* country." He sneezed. "You may rest"—he sneezed—"assured of that."

Unfortunately, a family of moths fluttered out of

the hole in his wig at that moment and orbited his head. The crowd in the courtroom laughed.

"Silence!" yelled Mr. Overbite.

"Silence!" yelled Shmink along with him, and they both sneezed.

"Ladies and gentlemen of the jury," the mayor continued, "and voters of the great coastal city of MacOongafoondsen. Do not be taken in by the urbane facade of this *Frenchman*. We know their ways. And if we don't know them, we can imagine them. I say this man is as guilty as—what, Mr. Shmink?"

"Sin," said Mr. Shmink.

"As sin," repeated the judge. "Do we really need to see evidence or hear testimony against him?"

Several cries of "Nay" were heard in the courtroom.

"I propose that the jury vote immediately," Judge Overbite said, "and I suggest the verdict be guilty."

A hubbub of general agreement arose, and Emmaline shot to her feet.

"Your Honor," she shouted, and was amazed when silence fell. "Your Honor," she repeated, "City

Statute forty-one says the jury may not vote until all the witnesses have been called."

"But City Statute forty-one-A says that rule may be suspended in a general emergency."

"This is no general emergency."

"As mayor," Mr. Overbite said with relish, "I hereby *declare* a general emergency."

"Hear, hear!" called some people in the crowd, led by Mrs. Overbite.

"We have a foreign invasion on our hands!" Mayor Overbite said somewhat hysterically.

"Yes!" more people called in the crowd.

"Who knows how many more Frenchmen could be out there waiting!" the mayor cried.

"Yes!" cried still more people.

"And what will they do? They'll pollute our community with their barbaric habits and foreign customs—just as this man has!"

"Yes! Yes! Yes!" Almost everyone seemed to be shouting now.

Emmaline jumped in again.

"This is an injustice!" she cried, stopping the hubbub. "You're only calling for a vote because you don't have a case! A flag doesn't prove anything. And my client couldn't have stolen a goose and a sweater and a cup, because he was locked into his cabin from the outside."

"Maybe"—the mayor fumfered a moment—"maybe he locked himself in *from the outside.*"

"How?" Emmaline demanded.

"By using"—the mayor thought a moment—"mysterious French self-locking methods."

The bailiff jumped in and scored a point.

"Maybe," he said, "the French locked him in themselves because *even they* knew how dangerous he was! Even the base, vile, sneaking French loathed and feared him!"

The crowd began to murmur again. Emmaline heard people whispering, "Even the French feared him! . . ."

"Your Honor," she said, "as you have no evidence, I demand you declare a mistrial. Or else I dare Mr. Shmink to call one single witness who can testify against my client."

"Very well," smirked Shmink. "I will."

Emmaline gasped as the bailiff proclaimed, "I call Jane Perth to the witness stand!"

14

Out of the Frying Pan

"Is your name Jane Perth?" Shmink asked.

"It is." Emmaline's mother looked baffled and uneasy sitting in the witness chair. Her eyes flew again and again to her daughter, as if seeking help.

"You have been housing the accused in your home?" Shmink asked her, pacing back and forth.

"I have been," Jane Perth admitted.

"Your late husband was a lawyer, was he not?"

"He was."

"He was a fair and honest man?"

"Very fair and honest, as you know."

"Respected in MacOongafoondsen?"

"Very respected, as you well know, Mr. Shmink," she said, then added fiercely, "And he spent his life fighting against injustice and cruelty, I'll tell you that!"

The pro-Eekers in the crowd cheered lustily. Shmink ignored the point with a crooked smile.

"Mrs. Perth, I would say that you yourself are an exceedingly fair and honest person."

Jane Perth said nothing. Everyone in town knew that was true.

"So answer me this, madam," the bailiff said, and stopped pacing and faced her directly. "What did you say to Peaches Cobbler last week, in front of the town well?"

Jane Perth said nothing, but a bright flush rose in her cheeks.

"Did you not," Shmink asked, "run into Peaches Cobbler in Only Street on Tuesday last and make a comment about the accused?"

Jane Perth maintained her silence, her cheeks now blazing a brilliant, shamed red. Her eyes went to her daughter, then sank to her lap.

"If you like," Shmink said, "I could call Mrs. Cobbler to the stand and ask her what you said."

"I did speak to her," Mrs. Perth admitted. "But

I didn't know Monsieur Eek very well at the time—"

Judge Overbite interrupted her. "I order you to answer the question. What did you say to Peaches Cobbler in front of the well on Tuesday last?"

There was a pause.

"I said," Mrs. Perth replied slowly, "that Monsieur Eek was always taking things."

"Ah-*ha*!" exclaimed the bailiff. There was an outcry in the courtroom. "Ah-*ha*!" the bailiff kept saying exultantly. "Ah-*ha*! Ah-*ha*!"

"But he always gave those things back!" the woman tried to say over the crowd's noise.

"He took *bright* things, did he not?" Shmink pursued. "*Shiny* things? Spoons and brooches and *cups*, for example? So might he not take a *gold cup* from the chapel, richly bejeweled with rubies and amethysts and emeralds and turquoise?"

"I object!" Emmaline cried out, shooting to her feet.

"Overruled," said Judge Overbite.

Shmink kept up his interrogation. "So this Monsieur Eek is a thief, is he not? Did you not say that to Peaches Cobbler in those very words? Did you not say, 'Mister Eek is a born thief'?"

"Yes," Jane Perth admitted. "I did say that."

"Repeat the exact words, please."

The woman seemed to sink lower into her chair. "I said that he was a born thief."

Even pro-Eekers looked shocked. Coming from Jane Perth, this was serious testimony indeed.

"Thank you, madam, you've been most helpful," Shmink said, then turned to Emmaline. "Any questions, counselor?" he sneered.

"Yes," Emmaline decided. "I do have a question."

The girl changed places with Shmink before the witness stand.

"Mrs. Perth," she asked her mother, "where does Monsieur Eek take his meals in your house?"

"At our table," her mother answered. "With us."

"Why?" asked Emmaline.

"Because," her mother said proudly, "I consider him my equal. *Our* equal," she corrected herself. "After all, he *is* a human being."

At that, a loud buzz filled the courtroom.

"Do you believe now that he's a thief?" Emmaline continued.

"No, I do not."

"Do you believe he's a spy?"

"I absolutely do not."

"Thank you, Mrs. Perth," Emmaline said. "You may step down."

Her mother took her place again among the spectators, but her testimony had been damaging. Emmaline surveyed the crowd and could see that some pro-Eekers had begun to doubt the Frenchman's innocence.

Now Shmink proclaimed, "I call Young Flurp the Town Fool to the stand!"

"Flurp? . . ." Emmaline wondered aloud.

Her friend avoided Emmaline's eye as he came up the aisle and took his place in the witness chair. Something looked strange about him today, but Emmaline could not put her finger on what it was.

"Your name is Flurp the Town Fool?" Shmink asked him breezily.

"My name," the young man corrected him, "is Philip the Town Crier."

Another buzz. Shmink stopped pacing a moment, taken aback by this response. Then he took it in stride and continued.

"Very well, Master *Philip*. A simple question. Have you ever had anything stolen from you in MacOongafoondsen?"

"Stolen?"

"Stolen," the bailiff repeated sarcastically, mocking him. "Improperly taken. Robbed. Swiped. Pinched. Pilfered. Purloined."

Flurp—now Philip—said nothing. And he still avoided Emmaline's gaze.

Shmink went on. "Did somebody not steal your famous rainbow cap last night?"

Emmaline now realized why her friend had looked so strange: He was not wearing his trademark rainbow cap.

"The cap is missing," the young man admitted slowly.

"Where and when did you last see it?" the bailiff demanded. "Did you not have it in your house, hanging on a hook, when you went to bed last night?"

"Yes, but—"

"Do you ever go anywhere without it?"

"No, but—"

"When you woke up this morning, it was gone?"

"How did you know that?"

"Never mind how he knows it," Overbite snapped. "Answer the question."

"Yes," young Philip admitted, "the cap was gone this morning."

"So," Shmink exulted, "it must have been stolen?"

"I guess it must have been."

"Didn't you always wear that cap to the Perth house? Didn't the accused see you in that cap daily? So mightn't he have wanted to possess it and taken it from its hook in your house?"

Philip saw that all was lost, and he turned to his friend. "I'm sorry, Emmaline," he said. "I didn't want to tell you. I looked everywhere for it this morning."

Now the whole crowd was agitated.

"Your Honor, there's no mystery about where that cap is," Shmink said. "I submit that the accused, Samuel Eek, sneaked from the Perth house during the night, crept into the Flurp—excuse me, the *Philip* house—and stole that cap."

Emmaline again jumped to her feet.

"I dare you to prove that!" she cried, her eyes flashing.

"You dare me?"

"I double dare you!"

"I accept your double dare," smirked Shmink. "Your Honor, I ask that the Court and the jury remove to the Perth house."

"Agreed!" rapped out the judge, and tapped the gavel end smartly. "Everyone follow me!"

Emmaline had a sick, sinking feeling as the courtroom emptied and the crowd poured out the door. Beside her, Monsieur Eek chattered and pointed and jumped. He wanted to go along with the crowd. When Emmaline joined her mother outside, the mayor and the bailiff and the rest of the citizens were already far up Only Street.

"What's all this about, Emmaline?" her mother said as they followed.

"I don't know," the girl admitted. "But I don't like it."

When she and her mother caught up, everyone was waiting for them in front of their shop. The bailiff said, "Mrs. Perth, will you take us to the room of the accused?"

Her mother led the way up the narrow stairs to the second floor. Emmaline now realized why they were there and what was about to happen, but she did not know how to stop it.

Upstairs, Mr. Shmink no sooner opened the door to Monsieur Eek's room than he cried out, "Ah-*ha*!" He pointed to Monsieur Eek's bed for all to see. "Ah-*ha*!" he cried again triumphantly.

A gold chalice and the rainbow cap were lying on the pillow of Monsieur Eek's bed.

"My cap! . . ." said Flurp.

"The cup!" said Minister Moonster. "But all the jewels have been pried off of it!"

Happy to be home, the Frenchman flew into the air and jumped onto the bed.

"No, Samuel!" Emmaline cried, but it was too late.

Eek set the rainbow cap on his head and flourished the gold cup over his head, waving it exuberantly for all to see.

"*Eek eek eek eek!*" he cried.

By now, the whole town had crowded into the tiny chamber.

"What's this?" the bailiff cried, snatching up a scrap of parchment. "A handmade map of the city of

MacOongafoondsen? Perhaps handmade by some foreigner, the better to spy on the town, eh? To search out our fortifications? To defeat us in war?"

The mayor turned to the others in the room.

"Ladies and gentlemen of the jury, I demand an immediate vote. Is the accused not guilty as charged? What is your verdict? Akmed the Cobbler?"

"Guilty."

"Miss Darkniss the Candle Maker?"

"Guilty."

"Tom and Tim Grognik the Twin Tavern Keepers?"

"Guilty."

"Guilty."

Every voice chimed in with the same verdict, some voices loud and firm, some quiet and disappointed.

"Philip the Town Crier?"

"I won't vote," the young man said.

"Shall the Court find you in contempt and jail you?"

Philip lowered his head and sadly added his vote.

"Guilty," he said, his eyes to the floor.

Only two dissenting voices spoke up.

"Emmaline Perth?"

"Not guilty," said Emmaline.

"Jane Perth?"

"Not guilty," said her mother.

The bailiff wrested the cup from the Frenchman's hand and whipped the cap off his head.

"Samuel Eek," Judge Overbite said, "you have been found guilty. Citizens of MacOongafoondsen," he said with arms wide, "what shall we do with him?"

The Mayor's wife now let out a cry: *"KILL HIM! EXECUTE HIM!"*

Others picked up the cry and started yelling, *"KILL HIM!"* Somebody else started a chant of "Death! Death! Death! Death!"

Emmaline looked around and could hardly recognize her fellow townspeople. There was Akmed the Cobbler and Ongka the Fat Bread Maker—people she had known all her life, but now transformed, their faces twisted with cruelty. Were these the same persons she had lived alongside all these years?

All the noise and excitement roused Monsieur Eek, too. He now jumped up and down on his bed and did somersaults, chattering along with the crowd.

"Eek! Eek! Eek! Eek!" he screeched.

"Do you see?" cried the judge. "He agrees! I call for an immediate sentence of death!"

The place grew deafening as people cried out for Monsieur Eek's death.

"No, no, no!" screamed Emmaline, but she screamed in vain.

"Samuel Eek," the mayor pronounced, "I sentence you to the full rigor of the law. Tomorrow morning, you will be hanged by the neck until you are dead."

"Eek," the Frenchman said, grinning and applauding. *"Eek!"*

"I order you, Philip the Town Crier," the judge said with satisfaction, "to cry this news in the street for all to hear."

Suddenly, the judge pointed to Emmaline and said, "As for you, Lawyer Perth, I charge you with harboring stolen property and aiding a thief and an enemy spy. Your own trial will take place one week from today. Be prepared for a similar verdict."

"No," her mother said. "No! . . ."

"Mr. Shmink," the judge commanded, "take Emmaline Perth and Samuel Eek into custody."

15

Into the Fire

There was no jail in MacOongafoondsen, so the bailiff locked Emmaline and Monsieur Eek in the chapel, where the trial had been held. When the shutters had been pulled shut and bolted on the outside, only the Eternal Flame at the front of the chapel provided any light.

"*Lawyer Perth,*" sneered Shmink the Bailiff. Then he went out and shut and locked the chapel doors. Voices of the citizens died away in the street. All was silent.

Emmaline looked around herself in the flickering, jumping dimness. The chapel's walls were a yard thick, the ceiling was twenty feet high, and the floor was age-old fitted flagstones, so there was no hope for escape. Soon, she detected the sound of hammering in the distance, and she knew what it meant: Barbara the Carpenter was building a gallows on the top of Edge of the Sea Hill. By morning, it would be finished and Monsieur Eek would ascend the scaffold and be hanged within view of the ship he had arrived in.

Emmaline sat down at the table where not long before she had pleaded Monsieur Eek's defense, and she cried. The tears came because she felt bad not only for herself but also for her friend, because she had failed to save him. The Frenchman himself seemed unaware of his troubles, though he could see that Emmaline was sad. He came and sat beside her, looking concerned and somewhat puzzled. Again and again, he stroked her arm with his strange wrinkled hand.

"They framed you, Samuel," she said.

The Frenchman just cocked his head to the side and said, *"Eek."* Then he chattered gaily in his own tongue, as if trying to cheer her up.

"I wish I could be as philosophical as you are," Emmaline said, her eyes seeking out the Eternal Flame. "I can't believe I thought I knew who was who. I can't believe I once said I didn't care if I lived among good people or not. You know what, Samuel? *Good* is *better.*"

"*Eek,*" said her friend, apparently agreeing with her.

"I wanted to be somebody significant. I wanted to do something important. Now all I've done is mess everything up." Emmaline sighed, following the hypnotic flicker of that lone flame. Strangely enough, locked up in that place with all hope lost, the girl began to feel drowsy. Long days and nights of study and tension had exhausted her.

She got up from her chair, stretched herself out right there on the stone floor, and almost immediately fell fast asleep. She dreamt that she was climbing up the side of Old Castle Rock. She was looking for something or someone, but she couldn't quite remember what it was. . . .

A soft rapping sound wakened her some time later—a knock at one of the chapel shutters.

"Emmaline? . . ."

"Flurp?" she said, sitting up. "I mean, Philip?" She scrambled over to the shutter and put her ear to it. Monsieur Eek let out a loud chattering cry, hearing the familiar voice outside. He had shrugged himself out of his blue coat and was scampering about in his usual way.

"It's me," Philip's voice said on the other side of the wood. "Are you all right?"

"I'm okay. I fell asleep. How long have I been in here?"

"A few hours."

"What's happening out there?"

"Well, Barbara the Carpenter is building a gallows. . . ."

"I can hear it."

"Your mother's talking to Mr. Shmink, trying to get you free. Emmaline, I'm sorry I voted like that. I felt like I had to."

"I know. But you got tricked. Samuel didn't steal those things. Shmink did."

"You think it was Shmink?"

"I'm sure it was. He must've taken the gold cup from the chapel, and he took the cap from your house last night. Then he waited till everybody was here and sneaked into our house and put them in

Samuel's room along with the map. That's why he was late for the trial. But first, he pried the jewels off the cup and kept them."

"I *am* a fool," Philip said. "A dupe. A dolt. A dunce. An idiot. An ignoramus."

"No, you're not. You're a good friend. A buddy. A pal. A true compadre. And you know what? I love your new name. I just have to get used to it."

"But why would Shmink steal Bob the Milkmaid's red sweater?" Philip asked.

"I don't know." The girl frowned, puzzled. "There must be a reason."

"The problem is, we can't prove he took any of those things."

"No—but if we could find those jewels—"

"Wait a minute," Philip said, interrupting her. "Somebody's coming."

"Philip?" Emmaline called. "Philip?" But there was no response. Then she heard the bar being lifted outside, and the doors opened, revealing Shmink. For some reason, Mr. Shmink was grinning. At least he was showing his pitted yellow teeth in an attempt at a grin.

"Thou art free to go," he said, adding sarcastically, "*Lawyer Perth.*"

"Free? . . ."

Emmaline started out the door, and Monsieur Eek along with her, but Shmink stopped the Frenchman. "Not you, sir," he said. "You stay here." He shut and locked the door, leaving Monsieur Eek inside.

"Why am I free?" Emmaline asked the bailiff.

"Ask your mother," the other answered cryptically. His breath seemed ranker than ever.

As Emmaline made her way home along Only Street, doors and shutters opened and people looked out to stare at her. All the pink-and-green banners and pro-Eek signs had been torn down.

Jane Perth stood waiting outside the shop, and when she saw her daughter coming, she rushed forward to meet her.

"Mother," Emmaline said, ignoring her mother's embrace, "why was I released?"

Her mother looked at her a moment, took a breath, then said, "I have agreed to marry Mr. Shmink."

"No, Mother," the girl cried out. "No! You *can't!*"

"'Tis true, my child," Emmaline heard. She turned, to find the bailiff standing right behind her, sporting a gruesome grin.

"Thy mother and I," said the bailiff, "marry on Sunday next. You will be maid of honor."

16

Partners in Crime

Mother and daughter argued bitterly all day, pacing the shop like caged animals.

"Don't you see?" Emmaline said. "Shmink framed Samuel."

"I know he did. But Samuel is one thing and you're another."

"No he's not."

"You're family."

"Samuel's family, too. Shmink probably made a deal with the mayor to get me accused just so he could get you to marry him!"

"Emmaline, this is the only way I could get you free."

Emmaline said, "I'd rather be locked up forever than see you marry Mr. Shmink. He's a lizard. A toad. A snake. A—"

Jane Perth interrupted, banging a hand flat on the table, her face livid.

"That's enough, Emmaline. I've agreed, and there's nothing you can do about it."

Without another word, Emmaline's mother went up to her room. Not long after, still sitting in the shop, Emmaline heard her mother weeping. The girl herself was all wept out. The idea of having Mr. Shmink in the house, handling her father's things and sleeping alongside her mother, nauseated her.

"Nothing I can do about it?" she muttered. "We'll see about that."

Quietly, she opened the shop door and peered out. Looking up Only Street to its far end, she could make out the gallows standing ready at the top of Edge of the Sea Hill. Shutting the door behind her, she quietly slipped around the corner. . . .

A short time later, Philip the Town Crier was marching up and down Only Street, ringing a bell.

"Evening in MacOongafoondsen and all's well!" he cried. "Evening in MacOongafoondsen and all's well!"

He stopped a moment and reflected, then

corrected himself and went about his job again.

"Evening in MacOongafoondsen and all's not all that well!" he cried.

"*Psst!*" Philip heard from some bushes. "Philip!"

He saw that it was Emmaline, hiding behind a rhododendron bush and motioning to him to come closer.

"Don't make too much noise," she whispered. "I want everybody asleep."

"Why?"

"Because you and I are going to find those jewels."

"Where?" he whispered back.

"In Mr. Shmink's house."

"Yikes," breathed Philip the Town Crier.

Soon after, the sun extinguished itself deep in the marsh and the inquiring owl awoke to go hunting. The tavern emptied and the evening chapel bell rang and all the candles went out in all the houses in MacOongafoondsen. Philip met Emmaline in the shadows under the chapel's apple trees.

"Should we let out Monsieur Eek?" Philip whispered.

"He'd make too much noise," Emmaline whispered back. "French people do love to hear themselves talk."

Monsieur Eek must have heard Emmaline's voice, because he started pulling on the chapel door and whining. Emmaline hesitated.

"I hate to think of him locked in all alone," she said. Monsieur Eek cried out even more. "Okay, I guess we'd better bring him along."

When they let him out, Samuel leapt into Emmaline's arms, crying *"Eek, eek, eek!"*

"Shh!" Emmaline whispered, and put a finger to her lips. Monsieur Eek put a finger to his lips, too.

"What's the plan?" Philip whispered. "The plot. The scheme."

"We sneak into Shmink's house, we find the jewels, you go up and down the streets, waking the town, everybody comes running, and Shmink confesses."

"Is that really a good plan?"

"No," said Emmaline. "It's the only plan I've got."

"If we get caught, we'll both get locked up—for good and forever, too."

"I don't care. I'll take the chance." She told him about her mother's impending marriage to Mr. Shmink.

"Yikes," the town crier cried quietly.

"You don't have to do this if you don't want to, Philip."

"Are you kidding?" he burst out. "For you?"

"Shhh!"

"I'd do anything for you!" said Philip, lowering his voice. "I think you're great, Emmaline-not-leen. I think you're marvelous. Miraculous. Stupendous. Unprecedented!"

"You can finish the list another time," Emmaline said, but she felt her cheeks prickling with pleasure. "We've got work to do."

A moon as white and bright as burning phosphorus had risen. They needed to move carefully. Creeping from shade patch to shade patch through the interlocking shadows under the chapel trees, they slipped over three fences and under a thorn hedge and dodged through several backyards to Mr. Shmink's house, which lay set back from the other buildings, as if those buildings were shrinking from Shmink. His house was a crooked and dirty old pile whose peeling paint gave it a lizardy, scaly, decayed look. All of its windows were dark. Emmaline and Philip sat watching it from behind one of the stinking heaps of garbage in Shmink's yard. Evidently, the bailiff disposed of his garbage by tossing it out his back window.

"Stinky," Philip whispered. "Reeking. Malodorous." Monsieur Eek covered his nose with his palm.

Emmaline jumped as something large and furry scuttled over her foot. It was a rat the size of a well-fed cat. The thing reared up on its back legs and glared at her with its opaque rodent eyes, hissing at her for disturbing its meal, then waddled away. Emmaline saw several other fat, furry shadows scuttling about in the garbage between her and the house and realized that the yard was filled with rats out for their supper. The squeaking rodents made Monsieur Eek uneasy, and Emmaline had to hold him to keep him from eeking. She motioned to Philip with her chin. They were going to have to move quickly and quietly through this brightly lit, junk-strewn space.

"One . . . two . . . three," she counted off in a

whisper, and they bolted forward on tiptoes toward Shmink's back door.

Halfway there, Philip's foot fell on a bottle and he slid and skittered forward. The rolling bottle flew up from under him and shattered against the wall of the house, exploding with a report like a pistol shot. Philip could not stop his momentum and kept windmilling forward, finally landing in a six-foot mound of junk that toppled under him with a deafening crash of glass and metal and wood and released a dozen more outraged rats, squeaking and darting everywhere.

A shutter banged open in the next house, where a lighted candelabrum appeared.

Emmaline grabbed Philip's arm and pulled him into a thin wedge of shadow along the house's back wall. The threesome stood hand in hand in hand in a tight line there, pressed into the gloom.

"Who is that?" Miss Darkniss called from the window next door. Rats were still scurrying all around, and over, Emmaline's and Philip's feet. "Filthy rats . . . ," Miss Darkniss muttered, and flung a piece of firewood into the garbage. The junk piles jangled all over again. Then the shutter closed, the garbage settled, and quiet fell again. Not a sound had been heard from Shmink's house.

"Do you think he's still asleep?" Philip whispered.

"I doubt it," Emmaline whispered back. "But we can't stop now. We have to find those jewels."

An open window lay right at Emmaline's shoulder, so she put a leg over the sill and slipped through the shadow into the dark house. Monsieur Eek followed her. Philip came last.

They found themselves in a foul kitchen whose walls and floor and surfaces were clotted with the moldy, stinking remains of a thousand rotted meals. It smelled even worse than the yard. This is the man my mother is to marry, Emmaline thought. He lives no better than a beast.

She put her mouth close to Philip's ear. "You search down here," she whispered. "I'll take the upstairs."

Philip nodded. Taking Monsieur Eek's hand, Emmaline followed a low, narrow hall until she reached a twisted, ramshackle staircase. She paused at the bottom step, looking upward and listening.

No sound. No snoring. Nothing. She turned to Monsieur Eek and put a finger to her lips. He did the same. Then she started up, placing her foot cautiously on each tread, but every step creaked under her weight. Halfway up, she stopped, waited, and listened. Still nothing.

At the top, she came to an open doorway and peered in. Moonlight coming through the shutters lay across a narrow bed, like fluorescent prison bars. Shmink was in the bed, under the covers, his hands folded over his stomach as if he were a corpse, his official dead-sparrow bailiff hat flat over his face. At the sight of him, Monsieur Eek started eeking under his breath excitedly. The Frenchman may have been philosophical in the face of death, but this man was his enemy and he knew it. Emmaline motioned to him to be quiet, but Monsieur Eek loped about unhappily.

Emmaline edged forward into the room on tiptoe, very, very slowly. Against the far wall of the bedroom, right next to the bed, was a chest. A perfect place to hide jewels. Step by step, Emmaline slid toward it, moving within a foot of the bed and the sleeping Shmink. Finally, she reached the chest, quietly grasped the knobs, and began to ease it open. . . .

"Gotcha!" cried Shmink, grabbing her arm and giggling horribly.

Emmaline struggled to pull away, but the bailiff held her fast, still making that low, creepy giggle. Then Monsieur Eek took a flying leap and, with a loud, screaming *"EEK EEK!"* landed right on the bailiff's face. The bailiff let out a scream and tried to claw the Frenchman off his head, spitting out tufts of brown French hair.

Emmaline yelled, *"Philip!"*

She grabbed Samuel's hand, tore out of the room and flew down the stairs. When she ran out the front door, Philip was right behind her. As the three raced up Only Street, the top shutter of Shmink's house flew open and the bailiff called, "Stop, thief! Stop, thief!"

Emmaline stopped at the town well. She could see candles being lit behind shutters in several windows. People would be coming out of their houses any second.

"Where do we go?" she panted. "We've got nowhere to hide."

"Yes we do," Philip said. He grabbed her and Monsieur Eek and leapt onto the stone edge of the well. He took hold of the rope holding the bucket, swung out onto it, seated himself on the bucket, and motioned the other two onto his lap.

"What are we doing?" Emmaline asked.

"Quick!" Philip said. "Get on!"

There was no time for questions. Emmaline and Eek climbed onto his lap, and Philip said, "Hang on, now."

Then he released the lever that held the bucket at the top of the well.

The winch let go, the crank whirled, the rope unfurled, and, sitting on the bucket, the three plummeted down the long stone shaft of the well into total darkness, screaming all the way.

They landed with a splash in frigid, inky water a hundred feet below. The great coastal city of MacOongafoondsen was now just a tiny circle of moonlight far above them. In a moment, that circle disappeared and they were floating in total darkness.

17

Underground

"Where are we?" Emmaline said, her voice echoing a hundred times all around her: *Where are we are we are we* . . . She struggled to keep her mouth above the water, trying to touch bottom with her toes—but there was no bottom. The darkness lay across her eyes like a clammy blindfold. "Where's Samuel?" she cried out. *Where's Samuelamuelamuelamuel* . . .

"It's okay, he's on my shoulders," Philip said from somewhere close by.

"Where are *you*? I can't see anything."

"I'm right here."

Emmaline felt Philip's hand on her arm and realized he was treading water alongside her. She seemed to be in a bottomless, lightless tank far below the surface of the earth—but the water in the tank was moving. A current was carrying her somewhere. She tried to control her rising panic, feeling herself tugged along helplessly by the persistent pull of the invisible water. This was just like one of her bad dreams.

"Where are we?"

"We're in a cavern," Philip said. "It's the tunnel of an underground river."

"But I can't swim!"

"I can."

"You *can*?"

"You won't sink. Just float."

"I don't know how to float, either!"

"Just relax. As long as you relax, you'll float. Let the current carry you."

"But where? Let it carry me where?" she cried. *Where where where,* her voice echoed. Fear overcame her, stiffening her limbs and making her sink. She thrashed her arms in vain against the unseen water. "I'm scared, Philip! I can't breathe!"

"Don't be scared," Philip said. "You can breathe. Just relax and you'll float. Be loose, be limp, and be calm."

Emmaline stopped thrashing, took several breaths, and did feel herself become more buoyant.

Monsieur Eek seemed even more panicky than she was, screeching in long, piercing cries, and Emmaline tried to quiet him.

"Put your hand out," Philip said, "and touch the cavern wall. Can you touch it?"

Emmaline reached a hand and her fingers came up against a steep wall of cold, smooth, sweating rock. "Yes, I feel it."

"Keep one hand on the wall. You'll feel better."

But it wasn't better. With her fingers brushing the wall, Emmaline could also feel how fast the wall was moving by. The relentless current was sucking them farther and farther down the tunnel.

"This water is freezing," Emmaline said. "My legs are getting numb."

Philip said, "I know this cavern pretty well. This is where I learned how to swim."

"Down *here*?"

"It was the only place I could learn to swim in secret. If people knew I was swimming, they would've thought I really *was* a town fool."

"Philip," Emmaline said, "where are we going? We can't go forever."

Philip's voice said, "It isn't too far."

"Not too far to where?"

Philip said nothing.

"Not too far to where, Philip?" she repeated. For some reason, he didn't want to answer.

"Well," he said, "there's another well farther down this river."

"What other well? Where?"

"At the old castle," Philip admitted.

"You mean," the girl began, "we're going to come up at the castle? At Old Castle Rock?"

"You don't believe in ghosts, do you?" Philip said. "You're a smart person. Bright. Intelligent. Rational. Sensible. Sagacious."

"Oh, be quiet," Emmaline said, but then Philip laughed and she laughed, too, and their laughs echoed like an audience. There was nothing else she could do but laugh. The current seemed to be moving faster now. The surface of the water bristled, then started to ripple.

"It can't be too far," Philip's voice said, though even he was starting to sound worried. "We just have to make sure we don't miss the place where the castle well drops into the river."

"What happens if we do miss it?"

"Well," Philip admitted slowly, "I don't really know."

"You don't *know*?"

"You've got to keep looking up. When you see the circle of moonlight up above us, that means we're at the well and we have to grab the rope that hangs down there."

"I'm too cold to climb a rope. I'm freezing."

"I just hope we get there before the moon sets, or we won't know when we get to the well."

They floated along, looking up all the while, for what seemed a very long time. Emmaline had lost all sense of direction in the dark and wasn't sure which way was up anymore. At one point, the river turned into a rapid and suddenly gave way beneath her, and she plunged over a drop and down a long water slide, even deeper into the earth. She decided she'd better keep talking, to control her fear.

"You know," she said, "I thought I saw somebody climbing up Old Castle Rock one night. . . . Or did I just dream that?"

"Maybe the castle is where Shmink hid the jewels and that's who you saw. Nobody'd ever go up there."

"Philip," Emmaline said, trying to make out his face in the darkness, "you're brilliant."

Suddenly, she felt him grab her arm.

"Look!" he said. "The moonlight! We're at the well!"

Emmaline looked up and saw a tiny wafer of pale light straight above her but very far away. But the current was pulling them faster now, and the circle of light quickly started to black out, eclipsing like a moon.

"Find the rope!" Philip called. "Grab it! Quick!"

"I can't find a rope!"

Emmaline's hands reached up and scrabbled for a line in the emptiness over her head, but her fingers grasped nothing but air.

"There's nothing, Philip! There's no rope!"

The cold current gripped her. She tried to slow herself by grabbing the wall, but the stone was too smooth and slippery-wet. Her fingertips scraped along it in vain for a hold. She imagined herself disappearing down the tunnel. "Help me, Philip!"

Philip's hands grasped Emmaline's collar. That slowed her.

Then she heard *"Eek eek eek!"*

Philip cried out, "Samuel's got the rope!"

Emmaline felt her body being pulled backward, against the current. Philip was swimming, tugging her back toward the castle well. In a few moments, that white circle of light appeared overhead again, with a thin black line of rope swaying upward against it. Monsieur Eek was climbing the rope toward the light, looking down at them to see if they were following.

"Wrap your arms around my neck," Philip said. "Hang on to my shoulders." She could make his face out now as a pale blur. She embraced his neck from behind, and he gripped the line and started to climb hand over hand, breathing heavily, grunting under the weight of two people in sopping, heavy clothing. Emmaline felt the river receding beneath her. Her knees, her calves, then her feet and toes rose out of the water. Then she was dangling over the underground river, hanging down Philip's back.

His breathing grew heavier and raspier and each pull up the rope took longer and longer. Then his hands slipped a couple of times, and every pull upward got shorter and shorter. They were still only halfway to the top. Emmaline could see Monsieur

Eek above them, at the lip of the well, looking down at them, whimpering. Then Philip stopped.

"I can't, Em," he gasped. "I can't hang on anymore."

Emmaline could now make out the side of the well. It was made of large, rough, unevenly laid stones, over which vines had grown.

"If we swing over," she said, "I can hook my feet on one of those stones. I'll hold us up till you get your strength back."

"All right," he panted.

"Swing," she said, and they moved an inch to the side. "Swing again." Another inch. "Swing!" Two inches. "Swing, Philip!" Three inches. They were moving from side to side in the well like the clapper in a bell.

"*Eek eek eek!*" she heard from above.

"Swing!" she cried, and suddenly her big toe touched a stone for a second. "Just one more! Swing!"

They swung over, and her toes grappled a hold on the edge of a protruding stone. They almost slipped, then held. She inched all her ten toes onto that tiny two-inch ledge; then with one hand she gripped a thick, rough vine.

"I'm standing," she said. "Relax your weight. I've got us."

Emmaline could not say how long the two hung there in the twilight of that vertical tunnel between world and underworld. She swore she would never be ashamed of her big feet again. What she did not want to tell Philip was that her own strength was giving out. Her toes were starting to slip. She started to sing quietly.

"Cowbells and bluebells and church bells
   Hear how they ring
   Cowbells and bluebells and church bells
   Hear how they sing
   Happy day, happy day,
   Happy happy happy day . . ."

Philip said, "Okay, let's go."

Pulling as hard and fast as he could now, he hauled them up without stopping so that his nerve did not give out. That wafer of moonlight grew and grew, until their heads were rising over the edge of the well into free air.

They were just below the winch of the well when they heard a *ping! ping! ping!* right above them, a strange twanging sound, and they looked up and saw that the frayed rope was coming apart under their weight, the fibers snapping one by one like fiddle strings. Only a few thin threads of ancient handwoven hemp held Philip and Emmaline up and kept them from falling back into the abyss.

Philip heaved Emmaline over the side of the well, then threw himself after her just as the long rope ripped and dropped into the well like a limp, dead snake.

They lay panting in the courtyard of the old MacOongafoondsen Castle.

"Well," Philip said, lying beside her, gasping for breath, "there's no escape that way now. I mean, if we needed an escape."

Monsieur Eek somersaulted several times for joy at being out of the well, then embraced them and kissed Emmaline and Philip's cheeks many times because they had made it out, too.

"The French," Emmaline observed, "do love to kiss on the cheek, don't they."

"I'd prefer a handshake myself," said Philip. Then they both shuddered, suddenly, with cold.

The ancient fortress sat naked on its high bare rock, and the wind that blew here was bone-chilling. Dead leaves and twigs swirled over the ground in whirlpools like twirling gray spirits. Emmaline Perth found herself in a fine situation: a fugitive from her townspeople, sprawled and shivering in darkness on the cold ground inside a courtyard of the castle where the crimson ghost of Angus MacOongafoondsen was said to walk.

The girl did not realize that she and her friend were being watched from a window in the castle tower.

18

The Crimson Ghost

"I wish we could get out of this wind," Emmaline said. Even crouching in the lee of the well, she couldn't escape the wind's razorlike bite. She held Monsieur Eek, who pressed against her shoulder, shivering and trembling. She got no answer and realized that Philip was scrabbling around the courtyard on his hands and knees. "What are you doing?"

"Looking for wood for a fire," said Philip. "It'd be better if we built it inside, though."

"Inside the castle?"

"You're already inside the castle," Philip pointed out.

"I'm in a *courtyard* of the castle. That's not inside the *inside* of the castle."

"Quibbler," he said. "Caviler. Sophist. Nitpicker. Pedant."

"Phrasemaker," she said. "Philologist."

The two laughed and felt a bit better. Philip gathered a pile of twigs and dry leaves, then dug a flint out of his pocket. Cupping it in his hands, he dried it with his breath, then struck it and struck it and struck it again. Finally, a feeble spark shot out, then another spark, then several all at once. The edge of a dead leaf caught. A minuscule blue flame appeared, shielded by Philip's careful fingers. It wavered, it smoked, it threatened to extinguish, then grew to orange and licked at another leaf. That leaf caught and set another leaf aflame.

Emmaline watched breathlessly, hungry for warmth and light. She found her thoughts racing forward through centuries, wondering if the world of future times would be brighter than this shadow-filled world of 1609. Would human beings ever be able to conquer the darkness and see their way around at night?

Philip's thoughts must have been going the same way as hers. "You know," he mused, "I bet if you put the right metal filaments inside a glass bulb and agitated their internal elements, you could make them glow and create light. You could call it—I don't know—a lightbulb."

"What a curious idea," Emmaline said. "To create light."

"Just a thought," said Philip the Former Town Fool. With the twigs starting to catch fire, he pressed a stick into Monsieur Eek's hand. "Samuel," he said, "could you find me a pile of these? Sticks? Branches? Twigs?"

The Frenchman just cocked his head, not understanding.

"Try saying it in French," said Emmaline.

"*Eek*," Philip said, pointing to the stick. "*Eek eek!*"

"*Eek!*" said Monsieur Eek, and swung up the castle wall on his long arms, somersaulting out of view over the top.

"My French must be getting better," said Philip. "Do you think everybody in Paris walks on their knuckles?"

Samuel returned with an armful of sticks and Philip fed them into the fire. As the flames grew,

Emmaline looked about and saw some broad stone steps leading up to the castle fortress, and a tower looming above it all. Nothing was ornamented. Every surface was hard, bleak, gray. The windows of the castle were mere vertical slits in the stone and looked like the slitted irises of a cat.

"I bet there's a great view from that tower," Emmaline idly observed. She could hardly get the words out because her teeth had started to click, and she couldn't stop them. She was shivering, too. The fire didn't seem to be warming her at all. Sitting close to it and hugging her knees, she shook violently from head to toe.

"You can't sit out here," Philip said. "You'll freeze to death."

"All right," the girl chattered. "Let's go inside."

Philip took up an armful of dry sticks and a couple of burning brands from the fire. Using them to light their way, he went with her up the broad steps to the fortress. Emmaline pushed on the round iron handle of the ancient oaken door. It screamed on its hinges.

Just inside, they found themselves entering the great hall of MacOongafoondsen Castle, a stone box fifty feet high and a hundred feet long, where their ancestors had met. Ancient tables and throne-like chairs were still here, blanketed in dust and strung with cobwebs woven by spiders as big as sparrows. Tapestries depicting gory hunting scenes and bleeding stags covered the walls. Rows of bats hung from the carboned ceiling like folded black umbrellas.

"Cheery," said Philip, ever ready with an adjective. "Pleasant. Jovial."

"Ugh," said Emmaline.

"Exactly."

Monsieur Eek seemed uneasy now, and kept sniffing the air as if he smelled something curious.

In one wall was a fireplace some eight or nine feet high, where whole oxen and deer had been roasted centuries before. Here, Philip laid the new fire, and they laughed at how pitifully small it was in that enormous hearth. But even laughing, the two looked over their shoulders uneasily. Both of them knew the legend of the crimson ghost of Angus MacOongafoondsen.

This castle had been the first home of the town, when thirty travelers washed up in the cove in the winter of 1143. MacOongafoondsen Castle had been here already, dating back to the days of yore, but was inhabited only by Angus, the last of a long line of powerful ancestors that had dwindled down to him. His lands lay unworked and fallow. His horses and sheep and cattle were dying off, untended.

Angus MacOongafoondsen was a rich, brutal, and irrational man who harbored a superstition, almost an obsession, about the number thirty. It dated back to when a soothsayer from Egypt had made an obscure prediction: *"Only thirty and MacOongafoondsen will prosper and thrive."* Ever since, XXX had been proudly emblazoned on Angus's shield and crest like a line of dark, loveless kisses. He began to see significant thirties wherever he looked. When Angus found exactly thirty travelers washed up below his castle, he took it as a sign: With this thirty, his family and lands would thrive again. But there was a condition: The thirty could live in the castle and work his land—almost as his slaves—but only thirty.

Strangers and wandering beggars, he turned away with threats. When a stray hunter once drifted

into his woods needing food, Angus MacOongafoondsen hunted down the hunter in the forest
and killed him. One of the tapestries here in
the great hall depicted the awful scene. His broadsword over his head, ready to descend, Angus
MacOongafoondsen had wide, crazed eyes and a
curdled, leering grin and looked curiously like a
brawnier version of Lexter Shmink.

Then two of the thirty conceived a child, and
on the day of the child's birth, Angus MacOongafoondsen gathered his company in the castle
courtyard. Legend has it that, standing on the top
step, he spoke to them thus:

"'Tis by my leave ye live here. 'Tis my law ye
live by, and my law forbids newcomers. I command
that this newborn babe be set out on the bare rock
this night and exposed to die by wolf or bear or
starvation."

When Angus MacOongafoondsen had said that,
the father of the newborn child stepped forward.
Everyone knew that in truth Angus MacOongafoondsen had desired this man's wife for himself
and that was his real reason for hating the babe.

The man spoke. "We stand grateful to you, sir,"

he said, "for having settled us here and given us shelter." Now he raised his voice in fervor. "But I swear by all that's holy that this my son shall live and grow here to be a man."

He pointed to an infant cradled in the arms of his wife.

"He only lives here," said Angus MacOonga-foondsen, "if one of us dies."

With that, Angus MacOongafoondsen drew his broadsword and advanced down the steps to meet the man in single combat in the center of the castle courtyard.

"Only thirty!" roared Angus. "Thus shall MacOongafoondsen prosper and thrive!"

The others formed a wide circle, and the new father drew his own sword. Though Angus had the better weapon, his opponent had the better mind and a quicker hand. The blades flashed and clanged, and the new father gave Angus MacOongafoondsen a deep cut across his chest, which ran with blood.

"Lay down your sword, Angus MacOonga-foondsen," the man said. "Yield to my son and the children of all who will live here."

"Never," said Angus MacOongafoondsen. Once

again, the blades flashed and clanged, and the new father gave Angus MacOongafoondsen a deep cut across his face, which ran with blood.

"Lay down your sword, Angus MacOonga-foondsen," the man demanded. "Yield to my son and the children of all who will live here."

"Never," said Angus MacOongafoondsen, and the swords flashed and clanged until he was all blood, a crimson man from head to toe, dripping gouts of gore that pattered in a scarlet puddle at his feet.

"Lay down your sword," the man said one last time. "Yield to my son and the children of all who will live here."

But Angus MacOongafoondsen simply turned and marched up the broad stone steps to the door of the fortress and stopped for one last time to address the crowd.

"You are none of mine!" he cried out. "I curse you all!"

With that, he went in and bolted and barred the great oaken door from the inside. He never came out again, starving to death rather than yield to time and this newborn stranger. That very day, the others moved off of Castle Rock, down to the site below Edge of the Sea Hill where the town still lay between the sea and the marsh. The father and mother of the newborn child raised him to a man, and that family's name was Perth. And the crimson ghost of Angus MacOongafoondsen, it was said, still walked the castle halls o' nights, dripping fresh blood.

The fire in the great hall was blazing now. Emmaline wasn't shivering anymore and her teeth had stopped chattering. She sat beside Philip at the hearth, looking into the flames and blowing her dried bangs out of her eyes. Her thoughts were continually interrupted by Monsieur Eek, who seemed uneasy, pacing about and constantly looking off into the dark at the far end of the hall, where stairs led up to the tower.

"Quiet, Samuel," Emmaline said. "Everything's going to be fine. You're safe now." She wasn't sure she sounded convinced herself. The Frenchman kept pacing.

The warmth and the presence of these figures had disturbed the bats overhead. The folded black umbrellas rustled and squeaked up there like thoughts.

"Where will we go now?" Emmaline asked Philip. "What will we do when the morning comes?"

The youth soberly studied the jumping flames, which were reflected in his eyes.

"I don't know," he said. "It's a great world out there. Of course, we could go anywhere. But where *is* that, exactly?"

"Thank you, Philip," Emmaline said simply.

The young man knew she was thanking him for saving her life, and flushed. "You taught me to read, I taught you how to swim. I guess we're even now."

"So you knew how to swim all along."

"That's how I found the ship. Sometimes in the early mornings, I'd pop down to the beach for a dip."

"You swim in the *ocean*?"

"Greatest feeling in the world. Quite refreshing in summer. A bit lonely, without company."

Emmaline gazed at him with open admiration.

"Philip," she asked, "does the world look different through blue eyes?"

"How could I tell?" he said. "They're the only eyes I've got."

"Sometimes," she said, "I like to try to see the world through your eyes. It's almost like I take a dip and swim around in them."

"How does the world look through my eyes?"

"Pretty nice," she said.

"Same world?"

"Same world. Just a little bluer."

Suddenly, Monsieur Eek let out a cry and dashed away out of the firelight into the dark.

"Samuel, stop!" Emmaline yelled, but the Frenchman had already disappeared up the stone steps at the far end of the hall.

Philip grabbed a torch from the fire and Emmaline another, and they took chase. But they were only several steps up the staircase when Philip stopped and pointed.

"Look!" he whispered.

Lowering his torch, he illuminated a gleaming drop of crimson on the step. *Fresh blood.* The two stared at each other a moment, their mouths agape.

"We can't lose Samuel," she said.

"You're right," he said. "Let's go."

They continued up the stairs, calling Samuel's name, and came to a crossroads: to the left, a corridor leading into the fortress; above them, the steps that led up into the tower. Ancient tapestries and banners hung here, too, among the ghostly furniture.

"Samuel?" Emmaline called. "Samuel! Where are you?"

"*Eek!*" they heard from somewhere above them.

"The tower," said Emmaline, and dashed up the treacherous, narrow, winding tower stairs, her torch held up ahead of her as she ascended the spiral. Philip was right at her heels. To their left was nothing but the empty space the spiraling stairs were wrapped around. The higher they went, the dizzier the drop down that central shaft. They were nearly at the top and Emmaline was just starting to lose her breath when—"*Eek!*"—she saw Samuel just above her, sitting and scratching his hand on a door at the top of the stairs.

"*Eek eek eek!*" he said. He was trying to tell her something about whatever was behind that door. He seemed to want to go through it.

"No, Samuel," Emmaline said, advancing slowly. "You don't want to go there."

She had just reached him and taken his hand

when the door opened and an icy wind froze her as a crimson figure appeared in the dark.

Emmaline screamed; then many things happened all at once. Monsieur Eek panicked at her scream and ran down through her legs, tripping her. As she fell, the torch flew out of her hand into the staircase's well, igniting an ancient banner with the MacOongafoondsen coat of arms. Philip caught Emmaline to keep her from following the torch into thin air. In the dim light, he saw the crimson figure descending on them, gabbling something at them, and Philip flung his own torch at the figure to drive it back. Grabbing Emmaline's hand, he stumbled in the dark as best he could, making his way back down the winding stairs.

By now, the fallen torch had set afire all the tinder-dry wood paneling and furniture below. Ancient chairs exploded into flame. When the pair reached the great hall, it was a blizzard of screaming bats and fleeing spiders. Disturbed by the smoke and commotion, the bats had flown down from the rafters and now swirled in the air. As Emmaline and Philip ran through with Monsieur Eek, the bats swooped and flapped and flurried all around their faces, and when Philip heaved open the oaken door to the outside, the smoke poured out along with them, and the bats as well, like ashes riding a whirlwind.

But Emmaline and Philip and Monsieur Eek stopped dead at the top of the broad steps. Below them, the courtyard was full of people, with Shmink the Bailiff at the head of the crowd.

"Chain the Frenchman until his execution," he said, and Monsieur Eek was grabbed out of Emmaline's arms.

"You two," the bailiff said to Philip and Emmaline, "come with me."

The castle blazed away behind them, eaten from inside out by flames.

19

The Gallows

When the sun rose the next morning, it gilded a gallows at the top of Edge of the Sea Hill. The gallows was not a very complicated contraption, just a crude wooden platform with an open door frame standing on it. A noose dangled from the door frame's lintel and an old stool sat beneath the noose. The person would be stood upon the stool, the noose would be fastened around the person's neck, the stool would be kicked away, the person would drop a few cruel inches, and—if the person was lucky—the noose would break the person's neck in the fall. If the person was unlucky, he would slowly choke to death, strangling on the end of the rope.

Around the scaffold grew the scattered violets and daffodils and crocuses that knew no better than to be there. A seagull occasionally landed on the gallows and studied the loop of rope with puzzlement. The bird's perplexity was not surprising, for in all the archives of MacOongafoondsen, there was no record of a noose ever having been tied in the town before Shmink the Bailiff tied this one. The undiscriminating breeze blew the noose just as it would blow any chestnut leaf or any shirt on a clothesline. The dew dried on the noose exactly as it would on a rose petal. The sea heaved and boomed in the harbor below, unconcerned. And a line of people snaked their way up Edge of the Sea Hill from the great coastal city of MacOongafoondsen, among them a young woman who *was* concerned, because on this fine morning, her friend Samuel Eek was to die. He walked alongside her on the end of a chain. Shmink the Bailiff held the other end of the chain, walking ahead of them as if he had Monsieur Eek on a leash.

"Eek eek!" said the condemned Frenchman cheerily, tugging at Emmaline's hand as if the two were headed off on another adventure.

"Oh, Samuel" was all Emmaline could get out. She knew that if she said more than that, she would start to cry. Philip walked on one side of her, her mother walked on the other, but Jane Perth did not hold back her tears. She had been weeping since her daughter was brought back down to town from the castle the night before. The ancient fortress was now a burned-out, smoldering heap of charred stone. You could smell the ashes from here.

The bailiff mounted the scaffold with Minister Moonster and Monsieur Eek. Mayor Overbite and his wife, who was wearing a fine black and gold lamé scarf especially for this patriotic occasion, positioned themselves in front of the gallows, at the head of the crowd. The bailiff stood Monsieur Eek on the old stool and fixed the noose loosely around his neck. It might have been the rope or it might have been the somber faces around him or maybe it was the queer silence of so many people, but Monsieur Eek started to look anxious, whimpering under his breath and looking about as if for help. No help was offered him.

Many of the people there, even those who thought Monsieur Eek guilty, felt uneasy at the prospect of watching him die. Many of them had watched parents and spouses and siblings and even children die. But what they were about to witness was something quite different. They were going to have to do the unthinkable: stand by and *allow* someone to die. Even Hammerklavver, who had been so jealous of Eek, found himself feeling queasy. Hammerklavver was actually a good and kind man, and, paradoxically, it was his love for Ongka the Fat Bread Maker that could make him cruel. Now he stood lost, not knowing what he should feel.

Shmink the Bailiff officiously whipped the blank scroll from his pocket and flipped it open.

"Samuel Eek," he proclaimed, "you have been charged and found guilty of spying and theft. These are capital charges, which means you are liable for execution. In accordance with this verdict, you are to be hanged by the neck until you are dead. Do you have anything to say?"

"Eek," said Samuel.

"I repeat. Do you have anything to say?"

"Eek."

"No?" said the bailiff. "Very well, then—"

The execution was about to proceed, when Emmaline spoke up from below the scaffold.

"I'll translate for him," she said.

The crowd parted to let the young woman through. She ascended the platform and stood next to her friend. He reached up a hand and touched hers, and she grasped his small, warm, rough hand tightly in her own.

"Eek," he said.

"In his language," said Emmaline to her fellow townspeople, "Samuel Eek says this: that justice is the science of being fair. He says, I have committed no crime. He says, I came to your city wishing evil to nobody, blown here by chance, just as your ancestors were. He says, *I exist*—which means I exist as much as you, Kawasaki the Left-Handed Farmer, or you, Onderdonk the Very Tall Woodcutter, or you, Barbara the Carpenter, who built this gallows. *I exist* means I smell these violets as you do, I see this sky as you do, I hear the ocean waves breaking just as you do, and all this is as real to me as it is to you. But in a moment only my dead body will be left here, and you will have robbed me of these violets, of this great blue tent of sky and this magnificent ocean. If justice is the science of being fair, then this is not fair. If mercy is the art of being human, then this is not humane. And the only crime in MacOongafoondsen is the one happening right here in front of you. This hanging is the crime."

Emmaline could not go on. Instead, she looked into each and every face there to impress her words on them, then crouched down to look in her friend's bright eyes one last time and gripped his shoulders in her hands.

"I'm sorry, Samuel," she whispered. "Forgive me."

She embraced him hard, then went down from the scaffold and took her place again in the crowd, but with her eyes on the ground. Her tears pattered on violets.

Mayor Overbite nodded to Shmink the Bailiff and Shmink nodded to Minister Moonster the Minister, who read a short prayer over Monsieur Eek's head.

"Now," said the minister when he had finished his prayer, "let us have a moment of silence."

Ages seemed to pass. The wind ruffled the water of the Great Northern Ocean. Birds circled and screamed. Then the minister said, "May God have mercy on your immortal soul," and Monsieur Eek looked about frantically as the bailiff tightened the noose around his neck. The bailiff had set his foot against the edge of the stool to kick it away, when—

"*Stop!*" cried a voice.

Several people gasped. They all turned and saw a gaunt, pale, barefoot figure of a man with lank locks of dark brown hair and a dark beard, wearing rags on his legs and a red sweater that had a spot of fried egg on its front.

"The crimson ghost," breathed Emmaline, recognizing him.

"My sweater," breathed Bob the Milkmaid, "with the spot of fried egg on the front."

"*Stop!*" the figure said again, raising a hand. "That creature is innocent."

Monsieur Eek had gotten very excited and let out a cry at the sight of this figure, whose voice had an accent no one in the crowd had ever heard before. Now he pointed his long arm at Shmink the Bailiff.

"Ask that man for what you seek."

All eyes turned to Shmink, who again moved to kick away the stool, but Minister Moonster stepped between and grabbed Shmink.

"This man?" said Minister Moonster.

"He took what you lost," the figure said. *"I saw him."*

"Buhh—buhh—buhh," the bailiff stammered.

"You took the chapel cup, Mr. Shmink the Bailiff?" asked Minister Moonster the Minister, his brow darkening. "And you took the jewels, Mr. Shmink the Bailiff? The rubies and amethysts and emeralds and turquoise of God?"

Now it was the bailiff's turn to point—at Mayor Overbite.

"He told me to take it," the bailiff said. "It was the mayor!"

"This is absurd!" the mayor sputtered. "This is libel! This is slander!" He pointed at his wife. *"She made me take it!"*

Just at that moment, Monsieur Eek took the opportunity to slip the noose from around his neck. Attracted by the gold-and-black scarf the mayor's wife was wearing, he leapt onto her shoulders and whipped the scarf from her neck, revealing a row of rubies and amethysts and emeralds and turquoises glinting like guilt at her throat—the chapel cup's jewels, fashioned into a necklace. In a second, he had tugged the string of gems from her neck and brandished them exuberantly over his head.

"*Eek eek eek eek!*" cried Samuel, jumping about.

"*Buhh—buhh—buhh*," stammered Mr. Overbite.

Emmaline leapt onto the scaffold. "I demand that this execution be stopped in accordance with City Law," she said.

"Which law?" demanded the bailiff. "Where is it written?"

"It's written *here*," said Emmaline, thrusting the blank scroll into the bailiff's face. "Canst thou not read, thou fool?"

The dead sparrow fell from the brim of the bailiff's hat.

Philip now walked up to the ragged figure who had interrupted the hanging.

"Sir," said Philip, "who are you?"

The stranger drew himself up to an imposing height.

"My name," he said, "is Miguel Antonio Unamuno de Parrìa. I am the pilot of the *Justice*."

With that, Monsieur Eek leapt into the man's arms and embraced the neck of his old friend.

20

The Stranger's Tale

Tim and Tom Grognik had a full house that
evening, as everyone in town gathered in their
tavern to hear the stranger's story—everyone, that
is, except Shmink the Bailiff and the Overbites,
who had been locked into Shmink's cellar until the
townspeople agreed what to do with them. The
Grognik twins were talking to each other again,
which meant they were dispensing their famous
pickled samphire and tansy pie as in the days of
old. No longer were the citizens divided into left
tables and right tables, and spicy buffalo turkey
wings and batter-fried goose wings were heaped
together indiscriminately in one great bowl.

At the fire, everyone sat gathered around
Miguel Unamuno de Parrìa, who sipped a cup of

hot buttered rum. He was not the pale, bearded figure of that morning, nor was he clothed in rags and Bob the Milkmaid's red sweater, which he had gratefully returned. Jane Perth had taken the man into her house, where he had washed and shaved. Emmaline had dressed his bleeding wounds with potions out of her father's medicine chest. Fully exhausted, the stranger had then slept the whole day through and risen at sunset. Now, after his rest and a meal, he was a handsome figure of a man for all to see, if somewhat thinned by his adventures, and ready to tell his tale.

"We were a hundred leagues off the coast when a storm blew up during the night," he began. "It was the greatest storm I have ever seen, and I have seen many. The *Justice* is a good strong ship, but the best ship in the world is nothing but wood and tar if not managed with a clear heart and a calm head. When the mainmast split, the men panicked and the call went up to abandon ship." He sipped from his steaming cup. All waited in silence, watching him drink. The fire crackled and hissed.

"When the storm blew up," he continued, "I locked my friend Samuel into our cabin so that he would not be washed overboard. For he is, truth be told, no great sailor, though he has sailed each of the world's seven seas."

"There are *seven seas*?" said Fierfl the Tailor.

"Seven, sir."

"And how many lands?" asked Kawasaki the Left-Handed Farmer.

"Seven great continents," answered the sailor. "I have set foot on them all, hot, cold, dry, and tropical."

Emmaline, who was listening at his feet, felt a flush of excitement rise in her cheeks from the thought of so many lands, and the fact that this man had seen them all.

"Are the French bad sailors, as a people?" asked Barbara the Carpenter.

"Every nation has good sailors and bad sailors," said Miguel Unamuno de Parrìa. "But how," he asked, "did you decide that my friend was a Frenchman?"

"By the French flag on the ship," said Hammerklavver the Blacksmith, and he produced the pink-

and-green-dotted banner. It was passed from hand to hand until it reached the pilot. He looked it over, amused.

"This," he said, "is a Chinese tablecloth. It covered the captain's table at meals."

Embarrassed looks were passed from face to face around the room.

"And Samuel, I am sorry to tell you, is not a Frenchman."

There were amazed outbursts on all sides. "Not a Frenchman?" "Not French?" people exclaimed.

"Actually," said Miguel, "I met him in a market in Lisbon."

"So he's a Lisbonian!" cried Onderdonk.

"You mean a Portagoose," Barbara the Carpenter corrected him.

"Well," began Miguel, "not quite Portuguese—"

"Who cares what he is," said one of the Grognika.

"He's welcome here," said the other.

"So the cry went up to abandon ship," Emmaline prompted, impatient for the rest of the story. "Samuel was locked in his cabin."

"Thank you, Miss Emmaleen," said the pilot.

"Emma-*line,*" she corrected him, and when Miguel smiled, she realized he had said "Emmaleen" to tease her, and she laughed.

"I was headed below to get Samuel," the pilot continued, "when a wave swept me from the deck and plunged me deep into the sea. Holding my breath until I thought I would burst, I fought my way to the surface. But when I came up, there was nothing but darkness. It was so dark, I hardly knew I was out of the sea. Luckily, when lightning flashed, I saw the main hatch floating within reach. If the thing had been two feet farther away, I would be dead now, but I climbed on and clung to it for my life. And when the morning came, I found myself floating alone on the surface of the Great Northern Sea."

"What about the *Justice?*" somebody asked.

"Vanished," the sailor said. "I thought the only scrap of it left afloat was the piece I was hanging on to. And hang on I did—for four days and four nights."

He paused now as Tim or Tom Grognik refilled his cup.

"So you're floating alone," Emmaline prompted, "on the Great Northern Sea."

"Floating did I say? Riding the back of a wild stallion is more like it, plunging fifty feet down and shooting a hundred feet up. Up and over and sideways I went, gripping the edge of the hatch until the blood of my hands attracted sharks that circled me. Then," said Miguel de Parrìa, "I saw your shore, and by God's fortune, the current carried me here to your village."

"City," said Akmed the Cobbler.

"Your great city," the sailor amended, with a bow. "This was not the first time I had been a castaway, so I knew better than to announce my presence. But I was starving and weak."

"So you took our goose," said Peaches Cobbler.

"For which," said the sailor, "I hope you will forgive me."

"And you took my sweater," said Bob the Milkmaid.

167

"Only because my shirt had been torn from my back," said Miguel.

"I would've lent it to you," Bob said.

"Ah," said the sailor, holding up a finger, "but consider what happened to my good friend Samuel when *he* arrived. Arrested. Accused. Condemned."

"Almost hanged," said Emmaline.

"Almost hanged," repeated the pilot, at which the entire citizenry, except Emmaline, looked ashamed. "So I betook myself to the shelter of your castle."

"Haunted castle," remarked Fierfl the Tailor.

"It has no ghosts, sir," said Miguel, "only bats, to whom I was grateful for company. As I was grateful to the castle well for freshwater and the surrounding woods for roots and berries. I also had the castle tower for an observation point. It was from the tower that I one day saw your Mr. Shlink? Mr. Shtink?"

"Shmink," said Miss Darkniss the Candle Maker.

"Thank you. I saw Mr. Shmink steal into the chapel and come out with its jeweled cup."

"Impossible," said Barbara the Carpenter. "No one could see that far."

"One can," said the pilot, "with this." He opened a leather scabbard hanging from his belt and took out a strange device, a brass tube about a foot long with a glass lens at each end. He pulled on it and the tube expanded to three times its length. "Something new from Italy. I got it from a clever fellow named Galileo. He calls it a *telescope*."

The thing was passed from hand to hand and tested. There were cries of amazement as people looked through one end, fixed the "telescope" on another person, and found that person suddenly close-up.

"As pilot," he said, "I carry my telescope everywhere with me, just as you, Miss Darkniss, carry your candles."

"So you're living in the castle," Emmaline reminded him.

"Yes, and during this time I had grown sicker. I could not light a fire, for fear I would be discovered. I was just about to make my presence known and ask for help when the morning came on which I heard your cry on the hill, Master Philip, and realized that the *Justice* had washed up. Through my telescope, I saw my friend Samuel arrested, so I decided it was wiser to stay where I was. I saw him locked up, I saw the gallows being built, and I was going to free him under cover of darkness last night when this brave young woman got there first and did the job for me."

Emmaline glowed as his eyes fell on her. Somehow that strong, gentle gaze reminded the girl of her father's.

"She is a person of significant character," Miguel continued, "and I pray you all value her accordingly. I heard her and her intrepid friend coming up the well last night, but kept myself hidden until I was sure of them. Samuel scented me out, they took chase, the castle caught fire, and I slipped away. This morning when I saw the injustice that was about to happen, I had to show myself. After which, I was taken in"—he turned to Jane Perth—"by this spec-*tac*-ular woman."

It was Gabriel Perth's own favorite word, and practically Gabriel Perth's own voice, come back.

Emmaline saw her mother smile for the first time since her father's death. The lively flush in her cheeks restored half her natural beauty.

"What about this woman?" Emmaline asked, holding out the oval portrait. "Do you know her?"

Miguel de Parrìa took the picture reverently in his hand. "My dear dead wife, Sofia. You have my eternal gratitude for finding this."

"What will you do now?" asked Kawasaki the Left-Handed Farmer.

"You might say I shall . . . *eke* out a living with my friend Samuel." The pilot smiled. "I have no home. I am a sailor from a family of sailors, so I must find my way back to sea." He noticed Emmaline's face fall. "Of course, we will return to visit our friends here. Indeed, ladies and gentlemen, I have a proposal for you all," the ship's pilot said, looking around the room. "I suggest that the great coastal city of MacOongafoondsen mend the *Justice* and launch her again on the seas."

"But the ship has no mainmast," said Onderdonk the Very Tall Woodcutter.

"You are a woodcutter, sir. A good length of timber will mend the problem, with the help of this woman," he said, turning to Barbara the Carpenter.

"The ship has no sails," said Fierfl the Tailor.

"You have a good deal of spare thread, I hear. And this man"—he indicated Minister Moonster—"is a weaver on secular days. With little trouble, we can weave a set of new sheets. You have a natural deepwater harbor here. Your city is a perfect port."

"With nobody to trade with?" Kareesha Kawasaki asked.

"The next city lies not two days down the coast. You might start there."

"How can we launch the ship without sailors?" said Emmaline. "There's none but you."

"Ah," the sailor nodded somewhat dejectedly, "there we have a problem indeed."

Just at that moment, the tavern door opened and a voice that no one there except Samuel and the pilot had ever heard before said, "Hello?"

Everyone turned.

In the doorway stood nine bedraggled men and, at their head, the captain of the *Justice*. Their lifeboat had just washed up in the natural harbor at the bottom of Edge of the Sea Hill.

21

Bon Voyage

Within a month, the *Justice* was drained and mended and recaulked, a new main hatch fashioned, the half-starved sea turtle set free, and the decks washed, sanded, and painted. Onderdonk the Very Tall Woodcutter cut down a very tall oak, which Barbara the Carpenter hewed into a mast. Plain Willum the Weaver removed the multicolored eight-foot ball of thread from the back of Fierfl the Tailor's shop and rolled it down Only Street to his loom. On it, he wove a set of magnificent multicolored sails. Hammerklavver the Blacksmith fashioned new metalwork for the ship while his new bride, Ongka the Fat Bread Maker, provisioned the workforce with fat biscuits and breads.

Building stones were scavenged from the old

castle for ballast to keep the ship steady. When he saw the castle stones, the captain of the *Justice* (who coincidentally had been an architect in Tibet some years before) realized that these ancient stones were a rare and valuable gray marble that could be traded up and down the coast.

Lexter Shmink, the ex-bailiff, and the ex-mayor, Ignoratius B. Overbite, and his wife, Lucretia, were set to work on board as deckhands and made responsible for swabbing, scrubbing, and hauling garbage.

At a town meeting, the citizens voted out black and gold lamé but were divided over what the new town colors should be. Just as an argument was about to break out, Philip rose to his feet with an idea: Since any choice of colors was bound to split the town, he suggested a *transparent* flag. On clear days, it would be blue; on cloudy days, cloudy. The idea passed unanimously, and on the sparkling day the *New Justice* was launched, the ship flew the new flag of MacDongafoundsen, which gleamed invisibly and flapped inaudibly at the top of the mainmast. Here is a picture of that flag:

Had you been at the launching ceremony, you would have seen Philip the Brilliant, mayor of MacOongafoondsen, formerly its fool, break a ceremonial bottle of Grognik ale on the *New Justice*'s bow to launch her. Philip had been the town's blue-eyed mayor for three weeks and took this occasion to announce that he was revoking the state of emergency and lowering taxes by four hundred percent. He also handed over the mayoral mansion to the Perth family in perpetuity, and ordered the Overbites to move into the former stable bordering the marsh at the far end of town. In the recent election, Emmaline Perth had actually been voted in as mayor, but she had stepped down in favor of her friend and runner-up so that she could pursue her legal and medical studies—after her trip on the maiden voyage of the *New Justice,* touching all seven of the world's seas and all seven great continents—hot, cold, dry, and tropical—and many cities of populations greater than twenty-one.

In these seventeen years since the *New Justice* was launched, MacOongafoondsen has witnessed many changes. The marsh has been drained, though the curious owl still asks *"Who's who?"* every night from the belfry of a new courthouse. Only Street has been lengthened and now branches off into Other Street, Third Street, Fourth Street, and Et Cetera Boulevard. All citizens now learn to swim at the age of six months. There is an annual Mac-Oongafoondsen Swimming, Sailing, and Diving Tournament, and the regatta at the new SeaWorld amusement park has attracted many tourists.

Miguel Antonio Unamuno de Parrìa, for so many years a wandering sailor, found a home in MacOongafoondsen. The affection that had sprung up between him and the spec-*tac*-ular Jane Perth blossomed into marriage. With her widow's shawl tossed aside, the careworn shopkeeper disappeared forever, leaving Jane de Parrìa-Perth laughing, arefree, and beautiful once again. She now lives a happy woman, the grandmother of two, overseeing her husband's shipbuilding business. That company has already flourished and launched several ships, among them one called the *Mayflower*. Some of the voyagers on that ship wore copies of Flurp's visored cap. Since then, the design has spread throughout the known world.

I myself can attest that all these things happened and are true as set down here, for I myself witnessed them. Indeed, it was I who stood atop Edge of the Sea Hill one spring morning, amid its daffodils, and with my fellow citizens saw a ship called the *Justice* on the sands below me. It was I who defended Samuel Eek at trial, and it was I who, with Philip, rode the underground river that still slakes our town's bottomless thirst. Samuel sits at my elbow at this very moment, cradling my second child in his arms, teaching her to speak "Portuguese" and checking my pages for errors. There, now—I feel his finger touch my arm.

I have written these events down as a record for my beloved husband, Philip, and my children, as a tribute to my friend Samuel, and as a public document for the archives of the great port o. MacOongafoondsen, population 947 and still growing. It seems the ancient Egyptian's prediction has come true after all: *"Only thirty and Mac-Oongafoondsen will prosper and thrive."* The soothsayer must have been speaking in prescient wonder. For a mere thirty people and a newborn child left Angus MacOongafoondsen's fortress and settled the land between a marsh and the sea, and out of them has grown a gracious people and a prosperous city-state—and the place in the world that I love beyond all others. It took merely those thirty, and a little time.

Signed on this her thirtieth birthday by

Emmaline Philip-Perth

Emmaline Philip-Perth
Chief Justice and Surgeon
General of MacOongafoondsen
July 11, 1626